# Tales of

# Questionable

# Taste

### Written by

### John Bruni

Coming soon from StrangeHouse Books:

**Murder Stories for your Face Meat**
by Kevin Strange
**Strange VS Lovecraft**
A Strange Anthology
**Tales of Questionable Taste**
by John Bruni
**Face Melting Pizza Freaks**
by Kevin Strange
**Grownups Must Die**
by D.F. Noble
**Apocalypse Meow**
by D.F. Noble
**Tales from the Vomitropolis**
by Jesse Wheeler

# TALES OF QUESTIONABLE TASTE

# JOHN BRUNI

## STRANGEHOUSE BOOKS

WWW.STRANGEHOUSEBOOKS.COM

"WHERE THE WEIRD, THE HORRIFIC, AND THE BIZARRE MEET THE STRANGE"

StrangeHouse Books
P.O. Box 592
Wood River, IL
62095

www.strangehousebooks.com

**ISBN-13: 978-1484025086**
**ISBN-10: 1484025083**

# Table of Contents

# The Space in the Bottom of Martin Oglesby's Desk Drawer

When Martin Oglesby dropped a full folder into his desk drawer, he did not hear the customary *fwump!* of the file connecting with metal. He had enough time to wonder if maybe the drawer was overstuffed—-and he *hated* cleaning up anything in his cubicle—-before peering in to find nothing. There was the usual assortment: a pad of paper, a half-empty box of pens, a couple of paper clips,and a handful of loose change.

But no file folder.

He closed the drawer and opened the one below it. No, it wasn't there, either, and it couldn't have gone through to the final drawer on the bottom. He knew he'd placed it in the top drawer. Where could it have gone?

There was nothing on the floor. If it had accidentally fallen into the garbage, he would have heard it. How could it have vanished? Was this a dream? He sometimes had nightmares about the office.

Martin pricked his finger with the staple remover. Not hard enough to draw blood, but enough to make him recoil in pain.

It wasn't a dream.

He opened the drawer again. Everything was as it had been a minute ago. Though there was no place the folder could have hidden, he decided to shuffle a few things around, just in case.

Martin reached into the drawer, but instead of touching anything his hand passed through the pad of paper and the box of pens and continued down until he was up to his wrist. There was no climate change. His hand remained the same temperature, there was no moisture, there were no variations at all.

Martin's stomach did a somersault, and he pulled back, half expecting to remain stuck. No, his hand glided out unhindered, and he stared at it, barely able to believe what had just happened.

"What's goin' on Marty?" It was Joe Brown. Every office has a guy like Joe. Instead of working, he goes around talking to everybody, relaying tales about how awesome he is, and laughing at his own pathetic jokes. No one ever wanted to talk with him.

"Uh, nothing. Why?"

"You look spooked. Gettin' enough sleep, Marty?"

"No. I mean, yes, I am, but that's not it. I . . . ."

"Something interesting in your hand?" Joe asked, smiling. "Like maybe a centerfold?" His laughter reminded Martin of everyone's favorite Stooge, Curly, though instead of being funny, he found the laugh to be smutty.

His inner debate over whether or not to tell Joe anything didn't last long. He looked up from his hand. "I have to go."

Martin slammed the drawer shut and walked away,

leaving Joe to stare dumbly after him.

As he wandered up and down corridors of cubicles, he tried to figure out who he could tell. Many came to mind, but none were free of flaws. Most would gossip about it later, and all would disbelieve him. A select few would even ridicule him.

Well, there was the new guy. He'd been here only a week, so he was still an outsider to the office's camaraderie. This made him the anti-gossip, and he probably wouldn't have the courage to make fun of him yet. Not only this, but the new guy had a habit of reading science fiction books. Earlier in the week it had been Heinlein's *The Puppet Masters*, and then he'd moved on to *The Day of the Triffids* by John Wyndham. Now he was on Asimov's *The Robots of Dawn*. Martin thought the man's literary tastes indicated a person with an open mind.

What was his name? Had he ever been told? The guy looked like a Lloyd. Maybe it was Lloyd.

No, it was best not to make assumptions. Instead, Martin approached the new guy's cubicle and said, "Pardon me, I was wondering if you could help me."

The new guy stuck a Post-It into Asimov and put the book down on his desk. "You're Martin, right? The guy in accounts?"

"Um . . . yes, I——"

"I'm Ray." The new guy offered his hand.

Martin gripped it momentarily. "Yes. Nice to meet you." He opened his mouth, waiting for words to come out, but Ray's introduction threw him off.

"What can I do for you?" Ray asked.

"My, uh, desk is broken. Could you take a look at it."

Ray blew his breath out and tugged at his collar, a living, breathing stereotype of nervousness. His eyebrows went up theatrically, and he said, "You came to the wrong guy. You need me to troubleshoot something? I'm your man. Fixing stuff? I'm terrible at——"

"Oh, no! No, what I meant to say is, I think my desk drawer leads to another world."

Ray stared at Martin's face, not saying a word. Sweat ran down Martin's forehead from the unruly nest of his balding blond hair. Neither spoke for a while.

"I mean, it's a portal to another world," Martin said.

"I understood you," Ray said. "It's just that no one has ever taken those words and combined them in that particular order to me before. Did that asshole, Joe, put you up to this?"

"Don't believe me," Martin said. "I'll show you. Make up your own mind."

#

Ray watched as Martin opened the drawer. When he saw its contents, he said, "It doesn't look like much of a portal."

Martin shook his head. "Never mind all that stuff. It's an illusion. Check this out." He reached into his pocket and pulled out a handful of change. After carefully examining every coin, he selected a penny and flipped it into the drawer.

There was no clatter. Ray watched as it vanished before hitting the bottom.

"Um . . . ."

"Yes, I know," Martin said. "Go ahead. Reach in."

Ray didn't hesitate; he dipped his hand into the drawer. When his fingertips touched nothing, he looked down to see what it looked like. His digits were gone up to the second knuckle. The border was clear-cut with no fog or anything to obscure his fingers, they simply stopped existing at one point.

He pushed his hand all the way down until he was up to his elbow. He then tried to look under the drawer to see if his arm was going through, but he wasn't flexible enough. Instead, he reached under the drawer and felt

**9**

around until he realized he should be touching the rest of his arm. When he knocked on the bottom, he didn't feel the slightest vibration in his other arm.

"Where does this go?" Ray asked. He stirred the drawer with his arm until he figured out the whole bottom was gone. He pulled back.

"I don't know," Martin said. "And I really don't want to find out."

"I do."

Martin blinked. "Knock yourself out."

Ray bent down for a closer look. His head would definitely fit in—-maybe his whole body, if he was skinny enough—-but it probably wasn't a good idea. Wherever the portal led didn't feel very threatening, but it was best not to take risks with the unknown. "Be right back."

When Ray returned, he had a cardboard tube from a paper towel roll. Without a word, he put one end to his eye and put the other into the drawer. He pushed down as far as he dared.

"See anything?" Martin asked.

"No. It's kind of gray, like the sky just before dawn. And I think there's some mist, too."

He was about to risk another inch when Joe slapped him on the back. "Hey Raymond, what's goin' on? You know I love ya', right? Like everyone does." He laughed too hard at his own insipid joke.

At the sudden movement, Ray accidentally dropped the tube, and it vanished. Slowly, he turned to face Joe. "Not a lot's going on right now. I'm just examining a hole in the universe."

Joe stopped laughing and cocked an eyebrow. "Drinkin' on the job, eh? Gonna' share?" He made a cylinder of one hand and pretended to drink from it, crossing his eyes. Laughing, he gently tapped Martin's shoulder and nodded his head back, as if to say, "You know what I'm sayin'." "You know what I'm sayin'," he said, grinning.

Ray grimaced, and for a moment, Martin thought he was going to go off on Joe. It was something he——and everyone else at the office——had wanted to do for years.

"Have you no imagination?" Ray asked.

"I got tons of it," Joe said. He paused for a three-count, then added, "In my pants!" He spewed more wretched laughter.

Ray nodded. "At least you're skinny."

"That I am. The ladies love it. You guys know what I'm talking about."

Ray, quick as a cheetah, grabbed Joe's tie clip and tossed it into the drawer.

"Hey!" Joe went after it, and both hands disappeared into the open drawer. He fumbled around for a minute, and when his arms went in deeper than they should have, he pulled back so he could look inside.

Ray squatted and grabbed Joe's ankles. Without ceremony, he yanked up so Joe's head ducked into the drawer. Ray lifted until it looked like Joe was standing on his head.

"Dude!" Joe shouted. "What the--?"

His voice suddenly became distant as Ray twisted, dropping one of Joe's shoulders into the drawer.

"Dammit," Ray muttered. He tried to control Joe's kicking feet while he unhooked the remaining shoulder. "A little help, Martin?"

It took a moment for Martin to realize what was happening. When he understood Ray's intention, he leaned forward and gave Joe a push.

After that, Joe's body sailed through.

"What did we just do?" Martin asked.

Ray wiped glistening sweat from his brow with the back of his hand. "Troubleshooted a problem."

"Is that a word?" Martin asked. "Maybe it should be troubleshot."

Ray shrugged. "It's not a verb I've ever considered

conjugating before, but you're probably right."

"Should we throw some food down to him? What if he dies?"

"So what if he does?"

Martin frowned. "That's a bit cold."

"Yep. Sure is."

Martin looked at Ray from the corner of his eye, and no matter how hard he tried, he could not hide a tiny smile. "I really don't care, either. I am afraid of what he might do if he comes back, though."

Ray nodded, biting his lip. "That could be a problem."

He grabbed the handle of the drawer and yanked back as hard as he could. The whole thing came out so far it popped off its frame and clattered to the floor. Its contents spilled out, and two quarters rolled in circles before coming to a jittery halt.

"It's a good thing I'm a troubleshooter, huh?" Ray said. "Hey, it works pretty well as a noun. Troubleshooter."

Martin didn't hear him. He was too busy experimentally waving his hand around where the drawer had been. When nothing happened, he reached down and touched the drawer.

It was solid.

"How'd you know that would work?"

"Lucky guess."

Martin nodded, scratching at his retreating hairline. "Where do you think he went?"

"I don't care."

"What if he's in a world filled with horrible monsters that want to kill him?"

"Then I hope they kill him fast," Ray said. "If they let him talk, the poor bastards are doomed."

# Outside Her Window, It Waits

It struck me on a basic level, and I thought, If cavemen could see this, they'd feel the same gut-chill. Yet the picture was so simple, it could have been done by a child. Drawn in Crayon against a white background was a blue window, clearly closed, as evidenced by the brown lines meant to be interstices. A pale, yellow moon hung behind these, only partially revealed in the frame. Under the window was a brown cradle in which a blue-blanketed baby wailed pink tears. Next to the terrified infant was a chaos of jagged black lines; it was some sort of shadowy creature with fierce red eyes and what looked like claws extending from the middle and resting on one side of the cradle.

"Do you like it?"

I looked up to see Esmeralda enter the room, wearing only a robe, lighting a Newport held between the second and third fingers of her left hand. An odd way to hold a cigarette, but she liked it. She said it made her feel different.

Still holding the picture, I approached Esmeralda and pecked her on the lips. "I love it."

"It's yours." She turned away so she could lie down on the bed.

"Thank you." I was very glad of the gift. I liked it a lot and intended to display it prominently back at my apartment. Taking one more look at the picture, I set it aside and eased onto the mattress beside her. Smiling playfully, I opened the front of her robe and caressed one of her breasts. It filled my hand perfectly—-no space, no excess—-and I gently squeezed. We looked into each other's hooded eyes, and I felt one of her slim hands at my crotch. Our lips met, and soon we were pressed together, rolling like a sea, wild and wet, exploring the caverns and protuberances nature had given us.

Later, as we lay side by side, her smoking and me just staring, she said, "It's true, you know."

"Hm?" The question was out of place, and I was trying to figure out if she'd been talking and I had just not been listening.

"The picture," she said. "It's true." She exhaled a cloud of smoke, and I watched it flow across the ceiling like mist.

"How do you mean?" I asked. As someone who didn't "know" art but knew what was aesthetically pleasing, I couldn't understand how a picture could be true, unless it was a photo or a recreation of a historical event.

I told her all of this, and she said, "It happened. To me."

*That's absurd,* I was about to say, but I bit my tongue. She was one of the few women in the world to ever fall wildly in love with me; without her, I'd feel lost, like a movie that didn't know how to end.

Essie had to have read some of that on my face. "You don't believe me."

"I didn't say that."

"You don't have to. That's all right, though. I know it sounds crazy."

I turned on my side and balanced my head on my arm. Tweaking her nipple absently, I said, "Tell me about it."

She didn't respond, not even to my fingers, so I stopped. "You can tell me anything," I said. "Everyone's crazy about one thing, at the very least."

She smiled. "Even you?"

"Actually, yes. Have I ever told you about the hand from under my bed?"

Her right eyebrow lifted, as if I was suddenly the loony.

"It's a true story, I swear."

"Then tell it, Seth."

I told her about how, when I was five years old, my favorite TV show was Dr. Who, and like most of my fellow fans, I liked Tom Baker best in the role. Desiring a thick, luscious head of curls like his, I started twirling my hair, under the impression that if I did this enough, it would eventually stay in place.

This was what I was doing as I lay in bed that night, so many years ago. My tiny knuckles brushed the wooden head board, beyond which, about a half-inch away, was a solid wall.

Despite the tight space, something managed to snake between the bars above my head, where it grabbed me by the fingers. I jerked and looked up to see, in the moonlight, a pale hand gripping my own and pulling. I screamed and yanked away from It, and the specter withdrew, back down between the bed and the wall, where no such hand could fit.

My mother came into the room and comforted me, and when I told her what had occurred, she froze and couldn't look me in the eyes. Years later, she told me the very same thing had happened to her when she, too, was five.

I'd told that story to several people, and when I

described the event to my brothers, a decade after it happened, two of the three of them said they had experienced something similar.

"Maybe you were dreaming," Essie said.

"If so, what about the others?" I asked. "They couldn't all be lying."

She shrugged. "It's a good, creepy story."

"What about yours?"

Essie took a deep breath. "Well, you know how long I've lived in this apartment complex?"

"As long as I've known you."

"Ten years, and in all that time, I stayed in seven different apartments. What I'm about to tell you took place in every single one of them."

"Well, what happened?" I asked.

She put out her cigarette in the ashtray balanced on my chest. "Sometimes, I wake up in the middle of the night, and I see that face—-" She pointed to the Crayon picture on her night table. "—-staring in at me through the window. It scares the shit out of me. Makes me feel like a kid."

"Seeing that at a window?" I said. "Hell yeah, that's scary." *Or crazy,* I thought, but didn't say. My stomach turned with guilt for even considering such a prospect, but I couldn't help it. Who could fault me?

"I kept seeing it," she said, "no matter where I moved."

"Did it only just stare?"

"Yes, but I think it wants to do . . . other things."

"Like?" As if I didn't know.

"I think it wants to rape me, but not like you think. It's more of a Linda-Blair-in-*The-Exorcist* kind of rape."

"Like, possession?"

"More than that," Essie said. "I think it wants to destroy me in order to be me, like hollowing out a pumpkin and putting a candle inside."

"But it only just stares?"

She bit her lower lip and chewed for a few seconds.

"Until I drew that picture. Then it started coming inside. I thought by illustrating it, it would be, I don't know, exorcised or something. I thought it would go away. But art only made it stronger."

Though I felt kind of silly, an involuntary chill puckered my forearms and nipples, and I hoped she didn't notice. If the whole story turned out to be a gag, I'd never hear the end of it.

"Every time I see it, it disappears," she continued. "I've been wondering what will happen if it ever catches me sleeping."

"Has anyone else seen it?" I asked.

"No. I had a few friends spend the night on more than one occasion, but it never showed up."

My first thought was for her sanity. Then, I wanted to comfort her. "Do you want me to start staying overnight with you more often?"

"I would, actually." She reached an arm across my chest and rested her head next to my neck. As I brushed a few strands of her hair out of my face, I could smell the lavender from her shampoo, and my sex leaped back to life.

"If it makes you feel safer, you can stay at my place, too," I said.

"That sounds good," Essie said, and we began round two.

From then on, either I stayed in her bed or she in mine almost every night. At my apartment, she never saw the creature looking in the window, and more than once, I stayed up late to see if I could see anything at her place.

Nothing ever happened.

Soon, we fell out of the habit, and her story seemed more and more ridiculous with each passing week. My boss switched me to the graveyard shift at the gas station, and since I thought Essie didn't need me with her at night anymore, I said yes.

The seventh evening, at one o'clock, I got the call. I

was chatting with one of the customers about the war in Iraq when the phone started ringing.

"I'll let you go," the customer said. "Good talking to you."

"Yeah," I said. "Have a good one."

I picked up the receiver and gave the customary gas station greeting only to hear a familiar, frantic voice on the other line: "Seth! Thank God! I need you!"

"Essie, are you okay?"

"No! It almost got me tonight!"

Already I'd forgotten the story, so I said, "Huh?"

"The thing at my window! I woke up just in time! It was reaching for me, maybe two inches away, when I woke up and saw him! He almost had me!"

By that point, I was convinced there was no shadow-thing; I was worried about Essie's *mind*. "Honey, I think you should—"

"I need you here, Seth! Please! If I fall asleep again, it'll get me!"

*I'm at work,* I almost said. Though it wasn't much more tactful, I instead suggested that maybe she should see a doctor.

"I'm not crazy!" she cried. "It was here! I know it! The window was open! It was shut when I fell asleep!"

I pursed my lips as I glanced out the front of the store. The station was deserted, and the chances of someone showing up for service were slim to none. "Okay, Essie. I'm on my way."

As soon as I hung up, I dialed my boss's home. No answer. I tried his cell, but it had to have been turned off. *The hell with it,* I thought. *He should be more accessible in case of emergency.*

I turned out the lights and locked up the pumps before getting into my car and speeding off for Essie's. When I got there, she cried in my arms for a while, and we went to bed, where we held each other until morning. Only then did we get some sleep.

The next day, my boss fired me. It wasn't as if I liked that job, anyway, but it gave me time to stay with Essie every night, like she'd requested. Since I was still on graveyard-shift mode, I stayed awake while she slept. Usually, I watched TV or read a book, and every once in a while, I'd look out her window. I never saw a thing.

Soon, we started doing things in the day again, and it got harder to stay up at night. A week later, I fell asleep in the middle of a silent movie on the Sci-Fi Channel. I awoke to a slight chill. Looking up, I noticed the window was open, when I know it had been closed. *Couldn't be,* I thought, looking over to Essie. She shivered in her sleep.

I decided she'd done it while I was passed out, as I remembered the room had been kind of hot before, so I got up, shut the window, and went to bed. Unconsciously, she embraced me, and I drifted off next to her.

The following morning, we had the first in a series of arguments. The subject, of all things, was the toilet seat, which I always left up. It hadn't bothered her before, but now she was crazy about it. In fact, it was a set of small details that seemed to upset her the most. Using her razor to shave. Getting water on the bathroom floor when I showered. Using too much butter on a pan while cooking. Leaving the TV on while I went to get a snack. Drinking the last of the milk without buying more. These were things I'd always done, but for whatever reason, she was only now going ballistic over them. It was like a stupid sit-com.

We seldom stayed together over night, and I was starting to wonder if being with Essie was worth it. The sex was still great, but every time I corrected one of my "little-things" errors, she always seemed to find more to scream about.

One weekend morning, after brushing my teeth, I couldn't find the cap for her tube of Colgate, and she detonated, blasting me with everything she had.

I couldn't take it anymore. "It's just a goddam

toothpaste cap! What the hell's wrong with you?"

She paused, glaring at me, but not a word passed through her lips.

"Jesus Christ!" I continued. "You're on my back about everything! It seems I can't do anything right! No matter how much I change to accommodate you! And it wasn't always like this! Why'd you change? How'd you become such a nag?"

"I'm a nag, am I?" Essie said. She lit a cigarette and gave me enough time to feel guilty about name-calling before she said, "Maybe you should just leave."

My anger got the better of me, and I wasn't thinking about how much I loved her. "Maybe I should," I said.

She shrugged and turned away from me. "Then go."

"Fine." I grabbed my clothes and my belongings. On the way out, I slammed her door.

For a couple of days, I stewed over this exchange, but not long after, I started missing her. Missing the way she felt against my body. Missing the lavender smell of her hair. I tried calling her, but she wouldn't talk to me. Every once in a while, I considered just going over to her place, but what would be the point? It was clear she didn't want me around.

A few months later, I found a new woman, to whom I am now married, but on occasion, I'd run into Essie's friends. They told me that after she broke up with me, she went off the deep end, hanging out with scumbags who turned her into a junkie and a whore, and she refused to listen to anyone when they told her she was self-destructing.

Last week, I saw her name in the obituaries. It didn't mention how it happened, but I was told it was a heroin overdose.

From time to time, whenever I'm drunk at a bar or party, I tell this story, and sad as it is, it always entertains, but I can tell no one believes the shadow-thing stuff. I wouldn't, either, except thinking back, I've come to the conclusion that whatever inhabited her body near the end, it wasn't Essie.

The last time I saw her, as she told me that maybe I should leave, she'd been smoking a cigarette. It was held between her *index and middle fingers.*

# Monster Cock

At first, scientists didn't know what it was. They could only see a speck in the distance. It got bigger by the day, so they determined that it moved toward us.

Years later, they developed better telescopes, launched them into space, and concluded that the thing had a snake-like shape, and its tail dragged on behind it for miles.

On the tenth year of study, they saw what it was attached to, and they couldn't get their minds around it. The data couldn't be refuted, though; a giant naked man hurtled towards us through space from a couple of galaxies over . . . and he had a raging hard-on.

They did their homework, made charts and graphs, and argued among one another. The guy had to be impossibly big, but no one could figure out a formula that would tell us *how big*. They managed to determine his trajectory, and the news was not good. His destination seemed to be our planet, and it would take him fifty years to get here.

The politicians wanted to keep this on the down-low, but the scientists panicked and let the world know. They didn't care about the consequences because they reasoned that in ten years, the Space Man, as they called him, would be visible on privately owned telescopes. Fifteen years after that, and any kid with a store-bought toy telescope would be able to see him.

The religious types saw this as a miracle, that the Space Man was really God, or maybe Jesus returned. They never talked about the erection, though, or what it might have symbolized.

Late show hosts turned it into a joke, probably on orders from the government. The big guy with the boner probably was not coming to us with good news, so why not lessen the threat in the eyes of the public?

The military didn't relax, though. They trained harder than ever and prepared themselves for zero gravity combat. Their think tanks worked double time for decades, and the best they could come up with was to launch nukes at the Space Man to intercept him before he reached our solar system.

The missiles got him out by Alpha Centauri, and they had no effect on him. After that, we sent a fleet of armed space shuttles filled with Marines out to see what could be done. No one came back. The scientists, observing from afar, couldn't tell for sure what had happened, but they think the soldiers tried to blast Space Man's dick off, so he destroyed them all with a single swipe of his hand.

After that, the human race became morose. We accepted that soon, a giant man with a love hammer the size of a bunch of earths combined would end our existence, probably with a cock slap. Hollywood made a movie about it, but they put clothes on the big guy and a team of rag-tag misfits saved the day. No one cared for it, really.

Soon, Space Man could be seen with the naked eye. Up close, he looked like a drunk who had just gotten out of jail. His long hair hung in tangles, and his beard needed a trim. The scowl on his face betrayed a relentless hangover, and his beer belly puffed out proudly, a cosmic accomplishment. His hard-on wasn't very proportional. If he'd been a regular guy, it would have come up to his chin.

When he missed us, the world celebrated. His legs went around us, and his balls almost thumped the north pole, but we made out okay. Scientists said that the movement had hurried the spin of our world, so days would be twenty hours from now on, and the moon was further away, so the oceans would be wild for a while, maybe forever, but we'd be fine.

And then, Space Man fucked the sun. He grabbed the base of his rod and jammed it into the center of our solar system. He had some wiggle room when it came to girth, but not much.

Everything went dark except for the little light around his hips. His ass clenched as he pounded the sun for all it was worth. The moans were enough to shatter all the glass on earth, but when he came, the sound of his whimper crushed mountains and reversed the flow of powerful rivers. Venus cracked in half, and Mercury swayed through the galaxy, nothing more than a rolling ball.

Space Man pulled back and with his flaccid dong hanging to his knees, he pushed off, probably looking for something else to hump.

Very little of the sun remained burning as it pulled the embers of itself into its center. Scientists guessed—-rightly—-that it was turning into a black hole. We had a couple of weeks before we'd be sucked in, but by then our atmosphere would be so useless that no one would survive to experience it.

The very next day after this announcement, Space Man's jizz rained down on us. It burst into flame on its way down, and it stuck to everything like napalm. Very few people made it through this; those who did could barely keep it together as they felt the planet move closer to the sun's remains.

Graffiti found at the end of the world: "We went out with a bang, then a whimper!"

# Amber

"I've just killed my husband. Pushed a shelf of parts down on top of him. I saw the rotors pop his head like a pimple, and I can't tell you how happy I am, but I haven't the slightest idea of what to do now."

The words rushed from her mouth like a tornado, and Mickey was sucked into her vortex, gnawing recklessly at mousetrap cheese.

## STEP TWO

This wasn't the first time Mickey had laid eyes on Amber Weston. He'd been a parts driver for the City of Redford for five years, and W&W Auto Parts——35 YEARS OF COMBINED EXPERIENCE BEHIND THE COUNTER!——-was one of his regular stops. Anytime Ford got stumped (and they were the only car company the City dealt with), his boss would send him to W&W, who rarely failed to supply the right stuff.

W&W stood for Weston and Weston, meaning Lou and Amber, the husband/wife team who owned the parts store juggernaut that served nearly every suburb in the area. Lou appeared to be a likeable guy, and he was very good at his job. Blessed with a photographic memory, he had every parts manual ever written memorized. All you had to tell him was the make, model, year, and part desired, and he could tell you off the bat whether he had it or would have to order it.

Maybe Amber wasn't as good at the job as her husband, but she knew her stuff, and she was a hell of a looker. There wasn't a man who stepped over the W&W threshold that didn't want her, and nearly all of them didn't want to screw with Lou, who was a six-four pillar of pure muscle, forged in the fire of hard work. Lou made sure everyone knew they weren't the sleek, useless muscles of a pretty boy yuppie by pounding any son of a bitch crazy enough to hit on his wife. It had landed him in jail more than once, but he didn't care. He lived according to his own moral code, and though he knew the law and submitted to its reprisals, he refused to let it dictate his life.

Unfortunately, he had a wife-beating habit. The evidence was as plain as day on Amber's face, but no one dared say a word--besides, what if they were wrong, and she was just accident prone?--and Amber never made a complaint.

Mickey, like a hundred men before him, was smitten with Amber. He looked forward to fetching parts at W&W just so he could say hi to her, to perhaps dissect weather patterns with her, to even find out how she is, how's life treating her. A few times, they'd even moved a little beyond small talk, stumbling into the realm of the personal. Yeah, my sister just got married. My father died last week. My girl dumped me. That's wonderful! I'm sorry. That's the way of things plenty of fish she wasn't the one time heals. Of course, when they said more than, "Nice day, isn't it?" Lou would pop out from the back room like a jack in the box at the end of its mad calliope tune, wiping sweat from his brow and grease from his hands, intent on making sure the talk was innocent. Amber and Mickey never gave him a reason to think they were making plans, so Lou remained a cheerful buddy, eager to talk about the Cubs (when it was Hot As Hell) or the Bears (when it was Cold As Hell).

Mickey wished she'd show some kind of interest in

him, especially when he saw her bruises, but he knew better than to butt into someone else's affairs. If she really wanted to escape, she'd call the cops. Besides, even Mickey was smart enough to realize what he felt for her was mere lust, really nothing over which to take risks.

Still, he thought about her a lot, even when he was off the clock. He tried to think of excuses to stop in on his own time, but nothing convincing ever came up. Whenever he was out drinking with the City mechanics--never anything stronger than beer, of course; Mickey remembered what whiskey did to him--he wished she was there, just so he could buy her drinks. Fancy meeting you here. What'll you have? Really? That's what I drink, too! On the few occasions he was able to talk a woman into his bed, he imagined he was with Amber.

Then came the day of her confession. He stood, silent as a man-sized sponge, absorbing the river of her speech, trying to figure out why she was telling *him*, of all people. It could have been any parts driver in the area.

He examined her pallid, blood-spattered Rorschach face as she explained her murderous act against a backdrop velvet mural of domestic violence. Her bruises were a roadmap to her tormented soul, and Mickey was shocked to discover he wanted to save her. Laughing Lou, always eager to share his opinion on sports and politics, a man who was quick to slap you on your back, and all this time, he had managed to disguise the baser side of his nature. Sure, everyone suspected, but most dismissed their thoughts as shadow-jumping. This was Lou, for Christ's sake! Yes, he had a temper, but it was easily understood, as he had a right to be angry at men trying to get into his wife's pants. Otherwise, he was a real swell guy.

Yet the truth still came from Amber's ever-expanding maw. Teeth the size of tombstones loomed over Mickey's head, her hole demanding him whole. He inched forward, feeling his white rabbit-form being sucked inside her. The roof of her mouth brushed the top of his head as he watched pink ridge after ridge pass before his eyes. How could he solve this poor girl's problems? How far could he fall?

"Let's go." The words sounded like someone else's, but he knew they came from himself.

And her mouth closed around him.

## STEP THREE

They were approaching Springfield on I-55 when Mickey realized fleeing the scene of a crime in a City vehicle probably wasn't a very keen idea. The thought was overridden by her appearance next to him. Her black hair swirled around her head, and as she drank from a water bottle with her lovely, thick lips, Mickey promptly thought about something else. It was shameful—she'd just murdered her husband!—-yet he couldn't help but wonder what she'd be like in the sack.

*I'm an accessory to murder.* The words echoed through his head. Suddenly, it became important to evade detection. If she went down, he'd certainly follow.

"I don't suppose you have any money, do you?" Mickey asked.

"Of course I do," Amber said, lighting a cigarette. "Lou had ten grand in savings, which he kept in a few Folgers's cans hidden around the shop. I always told the fool he should put it in the bank. Now I'm glad he ignored me."

"We have to ditch this pick-up, or they'll find us. We could probably get a good deal on a used car out here."

## STEP FOUR

They got an old Skyhawk from a stereotypical used car salesman named Sal, bad tweed suit, horrible cigar, and all, the whole gaudy display. Mickey left the parts truck by a cornfield, except he found abandoning it entirely a difficult task. He didn't know why, but he felt it necessary to peel the City decal off the driver side door with the aid of a pocketknife.

They got into their new car and continued on their way to nowhere.


## STEP FIVE


They stopped at a dingy motel halfway between Springfield and St. Louis. It was getting dark, and Murphy's looked like an anonymous place. The clerk didn't even ask for a credit card or identification. Amber flashed some money, and the clerk flashed the key.

When they stepped into their room—-#12—-they noticed it was furnished with a table, two rickety chairs, a television mounted on a dresser, and only one bed. Mickey bit his lower lip and laughed in what he hoped was an enticing manner.

"Well, I guess that guy thought we were a couple," Amber said. She smiled a little, speaking what he wished he could have.

*Why couldn't the clerk be right?* Mickey looked her up and down, devouring her outside beauty, not realizing he was more like Milton's Hounds, chewing at the insides of their mother, Sin. He spent so much time wanting to enter her, not knowing he already had.

"I can sleep on the floor," he said, hating every noble word that plopped from the anus of his mouth. Though he wanted to look at her, he stared at the carpet, where his feet shuffled, hoping she'd see through the nice guy to the sexual hunger beneath.

"That's sweet of you, Mickey."

It was the first time she'd said his name. His forearms puckered with goosebumps, and he felt the front of his pants stiffen. *Please,* his mind begged, as if she could pick up his mental entreaty via a psychic connection.

*Please!*

"We'll share the bed." She stepped closer to him and pressed her lithe shape against him, grinding her hips against his crotch. He felt dizzy as her eyes came so close to his it looked like she was a Cyclops. Her hair brushed against his face, and a maverick strand got caught in his whiskers. She allowed him to finish her advance. He gently touched his lips to hers, one moment chaste, the next French. He could feel her teeth behind her kiss pressing against his mouth, and he felt himself creep out the top of his jeans.

"You want me a lot, don't you?" she whispered.

"For the longest time."

Her hands fluttered down his chest and settled on the knob of his manhood. She unbuckled, unbuttoned, and unzipped him, unleashing his shambling beast upon her Bethlehem. Their molted clothes slumped to the floor, and their newborn bodies fell to the bed in a tangle. She greedily grabbed his sex and guided him into the Void. Sweat lubricated their gliding flesh, as if they were adjacent auto parts rushing against each other for maximum performance.

Mickey could feel her growing very sticky Down There, as if he had a wet piece of duct tape wrapped around his member. Though he'd only had sex ten times in his thirty years--not counting the times with his ex-wife, which he wanted to forget and therefore didn't count--he knew something was wrong. He looked down, pretending to be enthralled with his thrusts, and was shocked to find Amber's insides unfolding and rolling out each time he pulled back, not unlike a Chinese yo-yo.

He screamed, yanking away from her. There was a loud snap, as if someone had stretched a rubber band until it had broken. To his horror, he saw a piece of her still clinging to his shaft, no longer attached to the rest of her.

"What is it?" Amber asked through a mouthful of

shattered, jagged teeth. "Is something wrong?"

The features of her face, a face over which so many men had salivated, were now part of a lumpen mass almost unrecognizable, as if someone had taken a sledgehammer to her head. Bruises and blood covered her like a veil. Mickey couldn't handle it. To see such a remarkable beauty reduced to a battered mass was so grotesque he felt sick. Tears sprouted like limp weeds from his eyes, and his body shook from the horror.

"Are you all right?" she asked, and though he'd squeezed his eyes shut, he could tell she was slithering out of bed and coming closer.

"It's not me, er, *you,*" he said, thinking of the horrible D.T.'s he used to get before he started A.A. The others mostly saw bugs, but Mickey saw people rot before his very eyes. Now it was happening again, and he couldn't understand it. He hadn't touched a drop of the hard stuff in three years, five months, and twelve days.

"Did I do something wrong?"

His eyes involuntarily popped open. Maybe it was out of hope that it had been a trick of the light, or perhaps he simply had a perverse desire to look at her corpse-like visage, like a motorist eagerly rubbernecks a car accident.

Much to his relief, there was nothing wrong with her. She was as beautiful as ever.

"I'm sorry," he said. "I . . . sometimes this happens. I get attacks." Mickey, the picture of health, watched her eyes, waiting to see if she bought it.

Amber bit at his hook. She threw her arms around him, her soft body pressing against his hard, ugly features. "Come back to bed," she said, grabbing his now flaccid penis and pulling, as if he were a dog on a leash. Like a mindless collie, he followed at her side, but there would be no more sex. She tried stroking and sucking, but she might as well have been handling a sock.

"Do you want to stop?" Her fist still bobbed up and down.

He looked down at her, and Amber only offered dull eyes and tired hands. Yet another bane caused by excessive drinking: impotence. *But how can this happen without JackJimTurkeyEvanCrow, all my buddies?* He licked his dry lips as his heart soared with bats and his stomach plummeted like a rock dropped in a pond. Mickey never thought he would ever come to this conclusion, but Amber no longer mattered. As she worked the limp dough jutting from the nest of his pubic hair, he kept remembering her other face, the one that had been staved in.

No. He'd spent too much time trying to ride the monkey's back. Now, it was time to switch places, back to the way it used to be. Its claws sank into his shoulders, and it muttered its dark, chittering language into his hungry ears, two parts lover, one part manipulative bitch.

He pulled himself from Amber's grip and stood, searching for his pants.

"I'm sorry," she said. She rushed to his side, circling his work-rippled arm with her desperate hands. "Don't leave me. I don't know what I'd do on my own."

The monkey screeched in her face and battered her hands away with fingered feet. "I'm just going out. I'll be back."

"Where are you going?"

"Out. Alone."

"You *will* come back?"

He searched her face for any sign of rot. When he found none, he said, "Of course."

## STEP SIX

The clerk told him all the liquor stores were closed, but he always kept a little something for the guests.

"Whaddya got?" Mickey asked. His hands shook and tapped out a Morse code of need on the scuffed counter.

The clerk recognized the signs and smiled. Maybe he'd

be able to afford that plasma-screen television after all. He just needed thirty dollars more. "Normally, I have some Jim Beam or Evan Williams, but you look like you need something more . . . effective."

"Like?"

The clerk disappeared into the back room, then emerged holding a jar of clear liquid. "My uncle's finest." He cackled. "Fifty dollars."

It certainly wasn't worth that much, but Mickey didn't notice. "Put it on the room tab."

The clerk was wary of such a suggestion, but he knew an alkie when he saw one. Mickey would be back for more, unless he died, in which case the clerk would steal whatever he had in his wallet.

Mickey grabbed the jar. "Thanks."

"Have a good night, friend." The clerk mentally counted the money he would receive tomorrow, twice, imagining how the new TV would look on his wall. He thought he could sell more moonshine to the alkie, and he decided a pack of smokes would look great on his kitchen table with a sixer. Maybe he could even get a whore from Jimmie's Playhouse. Good times.

## STEP SEVEN

Mickey hid out behind the motel, where land stretched flatly into forever. The corn stalks danced and rustled as he screwed off the lid and sniffed the 'shine within. Nothing had ever pleased his nostrils more, not even the smell of Amber's canyon.

The first sip went down his throat, and he knew what Julius Caesar returning to Rome must have felt like as his countrymen celebrated Pompey's fall with a party. And then, as he slowly reached the bottom of the jar, he felt like Judas Iscariot arriving in Hell as the distant rustling turned to agonizing screams. Above him, galaxies whirled, just like the dust at his feet. The vast universe crushed him with a hellish claustrophobia as his memories howled inside his mind, threatening to explode from his head like Athena reborn. He could feel Satan's heat boiling the rubber of his boots, Its face trying to break through the ground and swallow him.

"NO!" He stomped the terra. "I won't let you!" He pounded the dirt with his fists, trying to beat Hades back into place, to scare the shades and devils away.

It never worked.

## STEP EIGHT

When he woke up, he could feel his demons pounding against the inside of his skull, and his mouth tasted like he'd been sucking a wet dog's rectum. He hadn't puked, as far as he could tell, at least not behind the motel, where he found himself gazing at a world distorted by the thick bottom of a twinkling moonshine jar. He could smell its former contents and knew what he'd done. Bile rose in his throat, but he swallowed the burn and tried to sit up.

*No wonder people hate me.* He thought back to his time as an alcoholic, remembering his friends and family. They'd tried to be supportive and forgiving, but Mickey had been too much of a drunken asshole. He was never violent, but the things he said tended to be ugly and raw. His wife and daughter kicked him out of his own home, and papers for divorce soon followed. He stayed with his friends thereafter until he systematically insulted every last one of them, prompting three separate ass-kickings. Only when he was homeless and getting his meals from college kids spooning out rations of soup, looking at him with sympathy and pity and relief--thank God I'm not him!—-did he realize his problem: Mickey was no longer an individual but a limb on Vagrancy's body. He was just one of a thousand Poor Bastards, with whom no one could identify unless they, too, had spent a night trying to keep warm under a newspaper while The Man "requested" them to get a move on no one wants to see a bum on a park bench get a job whassamatter with you?

Mickey had no name in those days; his life was so insignificant many decided he was a mere object, and the way he lived, he supposed they had been right. He could imagine nothing more humiliating than himself, so he started going to A.A. The YMCA offered him shelter and a place to bathe, and before long, he felt almost human again. Getting the parts job had finished the resurrection. As soon as he had enough money, he bought an old rustmobile in which he began living. His boss allowed him to park over night in the City Garage lot, and everything was looking up. He'd won back his name.

There was fear, however, of letting people get too close, close enough to see the ugly person he tried so desperately to hide. The extent of his social life was drinking (moderately, beer only) with the City mechanics every once in a while and the occasional one night stand. His heart begged for more, but he knew this was The Way It Should Be. His sudden relapse was proof.

"Good morning, Mr. Smith. Sleep well?"

He blinked and tried to focus on the man's face. It looked vaguely familiar, and a second later, he realized it was the clerk. "No, I didn't."

"I suspected as much, considering the complaints. You screamed quite a bit before collapsing last night. I would have called the police, but we have only one lawman, and he's out with the flu, except we all know he's really getting his syphilis treated."

Mickey shrugged, not knowing what to say to such useless information. What did John Law's syph have to do with his own drunken behavior?

"Got another jug o' juice, if you're interested."

Bile rose again in Mickey's throat. "No," he said, trying to ignore the sting in his mouth. "Hell no." He pushed himself to his feet and stumbled back toward his room.

The clerk watched Mickey's moonshine shuffle and thought, *That's fine.* He knew drunks always came back for more.

## STEP NINE

Amber wasn't in bed when he entered the room, and for a moment, he wondered if she'd decided to take her chances on her own. He jabbed a couple of fingers through the blinds and scissored them open. The car was still there.

"Amber?"

"In here." The voice came from the bathroom.

Mickey pushed through the flimsy, knobless door to find her inside the tub, mostly covered with suds. Her head was once more misshapen, and one of her eyes hung from the optical nerve, dipping into the water like a teabag. The bath seemed more like a stew of rotting meat. The sickness didn't conquer him this time as he examined her body. Gnarled, bony hands rubbed rancid soap across her peeling flesh. Now that he'd spent the night boozing, this image was easier to accept. How many people had fallen to pieces before his eyes in the old days? What was one more? Besides, it wasn't as bad as the time he watched his daughter drip away like a candle at the dinner table, the gooey corn and green beans she'd just eaten dropping to the floor through a hole in her stomach. He'd screamed and tried to put her on ice while duct-taping her injuries to keep her together. His wife hadn't been very appreciative of this, and though his daughter had been too young to understand it, she was so terrified she wouldn't come near him for a month.

"You hate me," Amber said. She looked at a festering hole on the back of her hand.

"No, I don't." It was the truth. Her decomposition had to be a figment of his boozy imagination; she was absolutely fine in real life.

Except he first saw her rot when he was sober, and though he'd had a hell of a lot to drink the night before, he was all right now. This should not be happening.

"Something disgusted you last night," she said. "Something I did."

"Don't be stupid. I love you."

"Do you?"

He didn't know. It felt like love, but lust did that sometimes. "Of course I love you."

"I hope so," she said. "I'd hate to think you killed Lou for nothing."

*Déjà vu*, he thought, but he didn't know why. "You killed him," he said. "I only helped you get away with it."

"You think I could push a shelf of parts down on him alone? That was very brave of you, coming to my rescue like that. I thought I had a Prince Charming on my hands. Last night, I found out you're really just another Wolf Man."

It dawned on Mickey what she was doing, and he detonated. "You think just because I'm . . . I'm . . . sick! You think just 'cause I'm sick you can plant these ideas in my head so I can take the fall for you? You're wrong! I'm sick, not crazy!"

She watched him a moment, regarding him with one good eye, still untouched by decomposition. "Are you sure about that? Do you remember anything about last night?"

Mickey's fists balled up, and for the first time in his life, he felt an overwhelming desire to hit a woman. He wanted to pound her so hard her face would peel off and stick to his knuckles like paste. There were, he knew, better alternatives. He turned and rushed out the door. This time, she wasn't curious about his destination, and she didn't wonder if he'd return.

## STEP TEN

The clerk handed over another jar of moonshine and smiled as Mickey eagerly accepted it.

He spent the rest of the morning until noon check-out time drinking from the jar and watching TV, which offered nothing good, except Tom and Jerry cartoons. When Amber emerged from the bathroom dressed, she was back to her old self again. He didn't let his guard down, not even as they settled up on the bill and loaded into the car. Not even as they ate breakfast in a greasy spoon. Not even as they crossed the Mississippi and into relative safety from the law. The moonshine lasted a while, since he wasn't guzzling it like Coca-Cola, as he had the night before.

The next three days went fairly well. Mickey stayed buzzed, and Amber remained alive. Occasionally, he imagined he could see a maggot crawling on her flesh, or nestling in the corner of her mouth. Ignoring it was no problem.

When he woke up in Oklahoma on the fourth day, he found himself bathing in a soaked bed. At first, he thought he'd been sweating profusely, but then he saw why. Next to him was the rotten mess that was once Amber Weston. He was covered in her fetid filth, and he gagged when he saw his hand had punched through her belly in the middle of the night, and his fingers were tangled in her rib cage. When he pulled himself from her, there was a squishy sound, and gooey strings of her insides stuck to his palms. Grimacing, he wiped her off him as best as he could and turned to the night table, where a bottle of Evan Williams awaited his grasp, ready to burn away his troubles. As soon as his gut was on fire, the ugly corpse next to him didn't nauseate him so much. Besides, he was getting used to her.

"Wake up, Amber," he said. "You hungry?"

"Mmm," she moaned, still half-asleep. She lifted her head, which was attached to the pillow by strands of corpse juice. "I could go for some eggs and bacon."

Mickey took three deep gulps from the bottle; he would need it to watch her eat.

## STEP ELEVEN

No matter how much he drank, she never looked normal again, and they were well into Arizona. By then, most of the rot had sloughed away, leaving dry bones with an occasional spot of greasy meat. He found it hard to believe this thing used to be a woman he'd put on a pedestal. More than once, he'd considered leaving her and heading home, maybe pick up the old parts truck on the way, if it was still where he'd abandoned it. He had the City emblem in his pocket, folded into a sticky square, and whenever he thought about Redford, he touched it like a talisman that would make everything better.

Soon, Amber was nothing but bones, and it was then Mickey really began to worry. Though she had no muscle, she was able to walk. Though she had no eyes, she was able to see. Though she had no guts, she was able to digest. He knew these missing parts—-in particular the spot between her belly button and thighs—-were integral to the acts she was able to perform, which made her existence impossible. Because he'd been sober when this began, he'd harbored hopes that, crazy as it seemed, her "problems" were real. Now he knew they were in his mind, and as scary as the supernatural was, he'd prefer that to his own insanity.

*his hands . . . parts shelf . . . rotors*

Not that it mattered much. He was getting used to her. This didn't stop him from drinking, which he now did every minute of every day. Somehow whiskey made everything good. Or sane, at least.

*didn't see her . . . not my fault . . . DON'T LOOK!*

It was because of this constant state of insobriety that it happened. They were driving through the mountains on a narrow road overlooking a steep drop into an arid land where rocks reigned supreme. Halfway through a bottle of Old Crow, he noticed nothing but the lines in the pavement ahead of him. Watching them pass and vanish under the hood ornament was the most exciting thing in the world. He wondered if it was really the road moving while the car remained stationary, kind of like standing by a creek and feeling a sensation of movement while watching the current glide by.

Amber's skeletal hand softly caressed the front of his pants, but Mickey was so far gone he didn't even notice. The road was making him dizzy, even a little sick, but he couldn't take his eyes from it.

"You all right?" she asked without vocal chords. "You don't look so hot."

Boozy sweat trickled down his back, and he remained silent, afraid that if he opened his mouth, he'd puke up all that wonderful whiskey, the Original Sour Mash, Aged 3 Years. It would be sinful to waste all that Kentucky Bourbon, even if it was rather inexpensive.

"You're breathing heavy."

He was, through his nose. He'd never open his mouth, not if he could help it.

"I can make you better." Her fingers worked at his zipper, pulling it down with a bit of effort. Her skull moved down into his lap, and her jagged teeth began scratching the sensitive skin of his sex. He looked down and could see her looking up at him, his member popping into view in her empty eye socket. Blood welled up from the gouges made by the bone job she was giving him, and suddenly it was too much. Something stopped in his chest, and a burst of air ripped itself from his throat, accompanied by half a gallon of Old Crow and chunks of truck stop cheeseburgers. This fetid collection from his insides sprayed all over the windshield, the dash, the steering wheel, and . . . he expected to puke on Amber, too, but she wasn't there. He checked the backseat, which was empty. She was gone, as if she hadn't existed.

Mickey's stomach dropped, and he realized he was no longer on the road. The world rushed past the windows, and he imagined he was Dorothy from *The Wizard of Oz,* riding the Kansas twister to another realm.

The fall wasn't as far as it seemed. The twenty feet of air only turned the car to the front, and on impact flipped it upside down.

Mickey was surprised to find he'd survived the crash. Nearly every bone in his body was broken, but considering his astronomical blood alcohol content, the pain had yet to hit him. Gingerly, he rolled out the front window, which had been reduced to a scattering of nugget shatter-glass. He moaned as he turned onto his back, facing a sun that beat like a heart, pouring rays of hellish heat down on him as if from a round, burning bucket. Gritting his teeth, he managed to turn away.

"Amber!" he moaned into the dust. "Where are you?"

Gentle laughter drifted down to him from the road above. He turned himself on his side and shielded his eyes. A woman stood looking down at him, and though he only saw her in silhouette, he knew who she was, and she was no longer a skeleton.

"I'm sorry," he whispered. "About . . . I didn't see the . . . ." What was the use?

Above him, she spun away and vanished.

Near his head, the plastic bottle of Old Crow sparkled, and he reached for it as far as he could. When he discovered his arm wasn't long enough, and sheer willpower wouldn't stretch it, and the Force was out of the question, he scraped himself forward across the shatter-glass and jagged pebbles until he was able to fit his hand around the neck. He spun the top off and began to guzzle the amber spirits. The plastic cover that made pouring easier made drinking harder, but he took it in stride. As long as the alcohol got in his system.

## STEP TWELVE

An hour under the sun, along with the remainder of Old Crow in his gut, caused fever to set in. The dry ground under him was the skin of a large desert beast, rising and falling with its gargantuan breath. Vultures swam in the thick air around the sun, breathing fire and blood as they kept their human eyes on him, waiting for the last breath to crawl out of his reeking mouth.

"You won't get me," he said to the devil. "I don't belong to you."

In his right hand, he clenched the empty bottle as he would a club, just in case the vultures got any ideas. In his left was the wadded up decal that had once been the City of Redford emblem. He found himself wishing it was a pair of ruby slippers. Tears streamed down his sunburned cheeks.

"I'm going to die," he said for no reason at all.

The skin of the beast split open and horned claws reached out to grasp Mickey's body. The vultures screeched their anger at having been robbed as he was pulled screaming into his Own Private Hell.

# Riding the
# Midnight Gloom

It's been either two minutes or two days since I eased the plunger down, and I'm watching the stars through my closed eyes. Even though the ceiling and the apartments above are in my way, it's like the Milky Way is hovering in front of my face. The floor beneath me changes shape to fit my form, and I feel like I am in the place where I belong. There is nothing in the universe that I want or need. I hold infinity in my palm; what more should I desire?

My lover is asleep. He doesn't approve of heroin, so I wait until he drifts off. We sometimes share our dreams, but not tonight. He probably knows what I'm doing; his mind is closed to me.

I force myself up into a sitting position, and the floor groans itself back into its original shape. My body does not want to move, but I manage to get to my feet and zombie-walk to bed. The air feels solid around me, and as I move, I can feel it caressing my naked body like a bundle of hands against my flesh. My foreskin rolls back, and I extend; it is the most sensate part of my body when I'm riding the midnight gloom.

I slip under the covers with him, pressing into his back, reaching around his hip to make him feel as good as I do, but he sleepily pushes me away. I drift from the bed and float down to the hardwood floor, where every grain embraces me.

It slowly dawns on me that it's happening again. I take to what I think are my feet and look down at the nearby coffee table. My kit is where I left it, and so is my body. I feel a moment of chilling fear, if such an emotion exists in this state, but I know everything is all right. My candles are not lit at this late hour, as they would have been half a year ago. As they would have been before I met Noel, my ex, the one who started me down this path. He was the one who told me that heroin sometimes makes you leave your corporeal body, but it doesn't do this for everyone. No, you have to be special. Noel was religious, so he believed it was God that made him extraordinary. I don't know if that's true, though.

Noel's no longer around. His body is, but not <u>him</u>. He passed through the flames and never returned.

Thinking about the candles makes me remember something else. I cast my gaze to every mirror in the room, and I relax when I notice I've remembered to turn them all toward the wall. No worries.

I hover over my body, and I try to lie down, to dress myself with matter once again, but when I try to sit up, I'm still not corporeal. This happens, and when it does, all I can do is ride it out until my body will let me back in.

It's time to play. I float out the window. The leaves of the treetops tickle my belly as I move through them. Birds scatter when they see me; they know I shouldn't be like this.

There are times when I feel I should check in on friends and family, to make sure all is well with them, but

I know I can't risk it. Some people have mirrors in their bedrooms. Still, I want to see Noel, or whatever is left of him in this world.

Instead, I soar higher and higher, beyond our atmosphere and toward the moon and the planets, where mirrors and fire don't exist. The astral tether won't let me go too far, but each time, I can stretch it out a little bit more. I want to someday see Jupiter's surface with my own eyes.

Below me, the earth is shrouded in a holey blanket of clouds; I cannot distinguish the continents. The moon blazes above me, full with the reflection of the sun. I feel like I can crane my head forward and kiss it.

Noel is the only other person I know who has shared this exhilarating experience with me. I've met my share of fellow junkies, but none of them have been able to leave their bodies. I think they are too scared. I tried to convince Steve, my current lover, to come with me, but he refuses to shoot up. He likes marijuana instead, as if that could offer these stellar sights.

I'm about to reach Mars when my guts, or what passes for my guts, constrict, and I feel myself falling back to my world, toward my body. I soar through my window, ready to join with my corporeal form once again, except it isn't where I left it.

When I see my body on its knees between my lover's legs, head bobbing up and down, I can't believe it is mine. Then, I see the joint in Steve's hand, and the Zippo he'd used to light it up. Flame. The gateway.

I try to push back into my body, but whatever is in there keeps me out. I bounce against my own supple skin, to no avail. Then, as if it senses my presence, it turns my own eyes toward me and grimaces around Steve's flesh. The thing sucks at him like one would suck a thick milkshake through a straw. I can see my lover's energy transfer into this creature, and Steve doesn't even realize it.

There is nothing I can do, but I keep trying to reenter my body.

Then, as if it has been expecting me, the thing holds up its palm, where it has concealed my shaving mirror. The trap. My astral shape screams, and I feel like I no longer exist. The universe pops out of my hand and moves into the creature's. I am alone, and infinity is dark.

# Virtuoso

If there is anyone in the world who knows what Vinnie Delva was really like, it's me. I wasn't there from the beginning, but meeting him in the third grade was close enough. No one else, except his mother (and squares don't count), was around him for longer, which is a double-edged honor. When he was good, he was the greatest guy ever; when he was bad, he was enough to make the Devil cringe. No in-between.

Though I can hardly blame him, considering how he was born.

His mother was a country girl, one-hundred percent. Looking at old pictures of her, I could see that any man would be lucky to bed her. Perfect body, perfect face, long, curly blonde hair that begged to have fingers run through it. Though she was a proud God-fearing, Bible-thumping Baptist, she loved the hell out of Elvis Presley. Not the mother-worshipping gospel singer, but the hip-flinging, hard-drinking rock 'n' roller. She'd do anything for the King, even break her own moral code of abstinence.

The rumors about Vinnie's father were started by her,

so why would they be false? According to legend, one night after a blockbuster performance in Atlanta, a pill-popping Elvis, long past his prime, was approached by young Miss Delva, and before long they were back-stage for an after hours game of hide the penis.

Nine months later . . . oh, yeah.

Fun little story. It's almost a shame she lied. "Almost" because the truth is even more interesting.

After Vinnie died, when his mom was in the hospital about to follow her son, she told me what really happened. It wasn't Atlanta but St. Louis, and it wasn't Elvis but an Elvis impersonator. She knew she could never have the real thing, and when she saw the pretender, he looked so much like the King (praise be his name) at his youthful best that she couldn't help herself. This was the closest she would ever come.

She was looking for a night of steamy passion and a lifetime of fantasies/memories. What she got was a relationship which lasted half a year. In that time, she learned his name (Doug Eckley) and his disconcerting past.

His parents were both mentally challenged, and they were brother and sister, just like their parents before them and so on. The doctor was surprised to find Doug born without defects, either physical or mental. He had an ordinary childhood, living on the edge of the New Mexico wilderness, where atom bombs were tested a mere two miles away.

How he cultivated his love of Elvis is a complete mystery, as he grew up in a house with no electricity, where his parents thought any music (including Beethoven) was the work of Satan. When he was ten, Doug was caught with a radio, and his father ruthlessly beat him with an axe-handle. In fact, throughout his youth, he received several such beatings, enough to make one think the Universe really, really, really wanted Doug to be just like his parents.

In one respect, he was; almost six months into the relationship, he pounded the hell out of Miss Delva (because she cooked his steak too well-done), so she waited until he was asleep, and she cut his throat with a garden trowel. Since they were living in a shack in the middle of nowhere, she didn't bother to hide the body. To this day, it might still be out there, mummified and staring at the ceiling with sightless, raisin eyes, wondering what the hell happened.

Miss Delva went home and told her mother that she was pregnant and the father had died in an accident. Her parents accepted her with open arms.

Then came the day Vinnie was born. The birth, as you can imagine, was a difficult one, and now that we know who his father was, we can definitely understand how he came to look like he did.

His head popped out, but after that, he was kind of stuck. Despite the sedatives, Miss Delva was screaming like a siren on a fire truck. Eventually, after poking around a bit, the doctor decided to go Caesarian.

When they opened her up, they were shocked to discover a baby unlike any other in history, past-present-and-probably-future.

I know many of you might not know who Vinnie Delva is. Some folks aren't too up on pop culture. I understand. In case you aren't even marginally aware of him, let me describe what the doctor saw: an ordinary baby in all respects . . . except, attached to his chest and left arm, like a conjoined twin, was a guitar. No, not an actual musical instrument, but a giant pad of flesh with six exposed nerve-studded tendons stretched across from his right nipple to his left shoulder and beyond. This bit of skin (with a cartilage frame) was how he'd gotten stuck on the way out of the womb.

Miss Delva wanted to have it removed, but it was impossible. His heart was inside that flesh-guitar where the sound box should have been, along with very sensitive nerves integral to his survival. So, the abnormality remained, and the legend of Vinnie Delva began.

For someone with such an obvious deformity, Vinnie had a pretty normal childhood, even though his mother never married anyone. Her parents helped out a lot. The only problem he had was as soon as he started going to school, fellow students were quick to make fun of him. This was swiftly brought to an end when Vinnie demonstrated his natural proficiency with violence. No one screwed with him after he broke Steve Smythe's nose and cheekbone. Suddenly, everyone wanted to be on his good side. He was in first grade.

Two years later, I met him. We were thrown together by the teachers because we had physical handicaps that kept us out of gym class. Because of the flesh-guitar, he couldn't move his arms very well. Because of my missing foot, I could barely walk, even with my prosthetic. We were relegated to the library, where we learned we had similar tastes (Hardy Boys, Encyclopedia Brown, Choose Your Own Adventures, and *Bridge to Terabithia*) and quickly grew to be close friends. In a week, we were inseparable.

We started hanging out after school, playing games and watching TV (we loved the hell out of Spectreman and Transformers). Occasionally, a friend joined our little group, a new kid who didn't know how to make buddies with normal people, but they never lasted more than a year. Some belonged to nomadic families and moved away; others managed to weasel into more popular cliques. Vinnie and I were the only constants, all the way through to high school.

It was there, during our freshman year, a music teacher by the name of Tune (which, I swear to you, is her real name; we also had a science teacher by the unfortunate moniker of Adam Boron) discovered Vinnie and his abnormality. She asked him if he'd ever considered playing guitar, which was a very common question, to which Vinnie usually responded with anger. It wasn't like he'd never played himself. He used to tweak his tendon-strings when he was bored, and though his flesh-guitar had no sound box, it still made music. He told me doing so hurt, like when you flex a muscle after a cramp, but sometimes his fingers couldn't help it. You see, in the early part of his life, he thought his deformity was a hindrance that would cripple him for life. This is what he told Mrs. Tune, who apologized and told him that if he ever changed his

mind . . . .

It took a beautiful drunk chick to do this and set Vinnie on the track to greatness.

We weren't invited to the party, but we thought attending would be cool, so we crashed it. There was plenty of beer, and it was our first time with any alcohol, so we were having a blast. Many girls we knew from class were dancing in outfits that barely covered their interesting parts (which was new to the both of us, as we were still virgins, go figure). It was glorious.

One of the cheerleaders, the hottest girl in school, fell drunkenly onto the couch between Vinnie and me. Now, in retrospect, she was probably being mean, but at the time, we were young fools thinking with little heads.

She wanted Vinnie to perform something for her. Well, demanded it, actually. "Play a kick ass song," she said.

"I . . . uh . . . ," was Vinnie's stunningly intelligent remark.

"Come on! You have a guitar attached to you! You gotta' play something for me!"

"Well, uh . . . ."

"Can you do 'Smells Like Teen Spirit?' Kurt Cobain is *so* sexy."

"I think . . . ." Vinnie started reaching for his strings. The rigid pad of flesh made for the perfect fret board as he tried to figure out how to place his fingers.

"If you can play Nirvana, I'll let you do me," she said with a crooked smile.

Vinnie cleared his throat and immediately started twanging his tendons. I saw him grimace at the pain as he started belting out a song that sounded vaguely like the anti-anthem for teenagers. His singing was awful, not just because he didn't know most of the words, but also because he was trying to sound romantic.

It was not good enough for her. "You suck," she said very loudly, and everyone started laughing at Vinnie. This sudden attention drew a contingent of jocks to us. Our asses were summarily kicked, and we were ejected from the premises.

The following Monday morning, on his free period, Vinnie went to see Mrs. Tune. His tutoring began the next day. Do you know what the first song he learned was?

You bet.

He learned music by Alice in Chains, STP, Soundgarden, all the teenage favorites of the day, even Pearl Jam (which he hated). It was during the annual talent show when he started gaining popularity. With me on drums, he proceeded to perform Nirvana's "Lithium" and STP's "Wicked Garden." The audience demanded an encore, so he did a censored version of Alice in Chains's "Man in the Box."

The minute he was off the stage, people who would normally go out of their way to poke fun at Vinnie were suddenly his best friends. We never had to crash a party again, just so long as the music kept coming. Thanks to my proximity to him, I was popular, too. When he started getting laid, so did I.

We rode the crest of this grand and powerful wave for the rest of his life, but I don't think he would have ever been better than a good bar musician without Mrs. Tune. She was the one who saw Vinnie's stagnant talent.

"You play well," she said, "but you'll never be great unless you start writing your own material."

This scared the hell out of Vinnie. He didn't consider himself very creative, but he took Mrs. Tune's words to heart. At first, his songs were pale imitations of the bands of the day, but as he got older, he got better until you couldn't even see his influences in his work.

Most importantly, everyone loved his music.

Instead of going to college like I did, he hit the road, playing bars all over the country with a few friends from high school as his back-up band. His agent found him in an Arizona roadhouse, and soon he had a record deal. Vinnie wasn't even twenty.

I don't think I have to talk about this part of his story. Everyone knows it. The concerts, the videos, the awards, the movie appearances, the legendary G4 performance, the time he rocked out with Jerry Cantrell and Les Claypool, you're familiar with all this. If not, check out one of the many biographies. *Playing My Skin* by Kurt Loder is the best of them.

Fame and riches did wonders for Vinnie. He took care of his friends. When I had to have my appendix removed (without the aid of insurance), he paid for it. He gave me the money to pay off my student loan. When my car died on me, he bought a new one. I never asked him to do any of this, but he did it all the same, and I'll be forever grateful. He was the best friend I ever had.

But his career was not all fun and paid off student loans. He developed an incredible ego which was at its worst when he was drunk. He made unreasonable demands, he didn't tolerate anyone taking the focus from him, and on several coked-up nights, he hit women. One sued him, and since he was sober when the papers were served, he paid up and apologized profusely. It doesn't make what he did right, and I made sure he understood this, but despite the ugliest corners of his Soul of Many Colors, he was my friend.

Which is why it hurts me to write this next part. No one knows why he dropped out of the lime-light, and no one knows how he died a year and a half later . . . except for me.

Vinnie was drunk and belligerent on the night his shooting star fame fell into the ocean of obscurity. The catalyst? The same that had started him on his way: a beautiful drunk girl.

At the end of a show in Knoxville, he invited the female in question backstage, and just like all his other women fans that had received this offer, she accepted without a second thought. There was, unfortunately, a problem: she had a boyfriend, and he got out of the bathroom just in time to see her being led away by Vinnie.

Jason Kells had every right to be pissed off, but I wish he'd just swallowed his pride and walked away. Instead, he ran after them, broke a security guard's nose, and tried to take his girl, one Steff Jensen, back.

If it had happened pre-fame, Vinnie would have apologized and said he didn't know she was taken. When he became a widely-popular musician, his ego had blown his head up enough to make GWAR's Skullhedface nervous. In Vinnie's old age, he decided to tell Mr. Kells off and proceeded to remove Ms. Jensen backstage, where he intended to do exactly what his father had done with his mother all those years ago.

Mr. Kells informed Vinnie that he didn't appreciate my friend's tone (which was a lot more vulgar than I'm saying here), and he threw a punch. Later, Mr. Kells notified the police he was aiming for Vinnie's face, but he was drunk. Instead, the fist connected with the neck of Vinnie's flesh-guitar, which broke with a tremendous crack. All six strings snapped and coiled at the bottom of his chest.

I had never heard such a scream in my life as the one that came from Vinnie that night. I'd been on my way to the stage to back up my friend (the going was slow, even with the new prosthetic Vinnie had bought for me), but when I saw I was too late, I pulled myself up over the speakers and hit Mr. Kells on the jaw, knocking him to the floor and giving him a concussion. When I was sure he wasn't going to get up, I went to Vinnie's side and stayed with him until the paramedics arrived.

No matter how much money he had, the doctors said there was no way the flesh-guitar could be fixed. They had to remove the broken fret board, but the sound box would have to remain in place, as that was where his heart was.

As far as the public was concerned, Vinnie fell off the face of the earth. To his mother and me, he became our life. His depression was so terrible we had to keep an eye on him at all times. Drinking was okay, but only in moderation (not that he paid us mind; he was good at sneaking booze). He became a much different kind of jerk, one with no ego whatsoever. Everything he said was bitter. Dismal thoughts kept popping out of his mouth. Nothing could make him feel better.

The money started drying up, and with it went his so-called friends. All that remained was me, just like when we were kids. Not even the guys at BLENDER and ROLLING STONE tried meeting with him anymore.

Vinnie didn't live long enough to see the where-is-he-now? segment on E!'s news show. A year and a half after his final concert, he was found dead in his bedroom by his mother. It was reported as a suicide, and I suppose this was true.

What no one except me and the cops knew (until now) was *how*, though I'm sure after having read this, you can probably guess.

Here he was, at the end of his life, in the same position as he was in third grade; his deformity was nothing more than a nuisance now. There was no use for it, since it was broken. Vinnie had tried playing actual guitars, but he could never master them. This pad of flesh on his chest and the stub of cartilage on his shoulder were a reminder of how crippled his life truly was.

Since the doctors refused to remove it, Vinnie did it himself with a Ginsu knife. I like to think he survived a few minutes afterward, just long enough to be happy at being normal, but he probably didn't make it through the self-surgery. Most likely, he died the instant he cut into his heart.

I miss him, and I know I'm not the only one. There are still websites devoted to him (and more than a few that subscribe to the conspiracy theory that he's still alive; he's not, by the way; I was at his funeral), and not too long ago, a Vinnie Delva tribute album came out, produced by Buckethead.

I think this is why there were rumors about Elvis's continual mystery-shrouded survival. The man was clearly dead (if he wasn't, why did he arrange to "die," of all places, on something as embarrassing as a toilet?), but he'd left his music behind. It wasn't like all his songs suddenly vanished off every record and eight-track the second he passed on. If anything, his music is more abundant now than ever.

So, what the hell? Vinnie Delva's alive. I hear him every day, and chances are, so do you. Long live rock.

# Suicidal Tendencies (with Nicole Evans)

Jake checked his watch. 1:13 in the morning. He knew she should be done by now, but he forced himself to wait two more minutes before pulling himself away from *Leaving Las Vegas*. During this last moment, his eyes alternated between the movie and his plastic-covered feet. Before he got up, he made sure the bags were securely fastened around his ankles. He refrained from touching anything with his hands as he pushed the bathroom door open with his foot.

There she was, staring up at him with empty eyes. Her body was pleasantly relaxed in the thick red curds of her own life. Her blood gently caressed the walls of the bathtub, and there on the rim were the razor blades, resting in streaks of red. Although he couldn't see the cuts on her arms, he knew they were there. He'd watched her do it.

"Anne," he whispered. There was no response. She was definitely gone.

He went through the "evidence" once again: a closet full of black clothing, a CD collection filled with depressing music and albums written by people who had killed themselves, and woeful movies on the coffee table. In the DVD player, he left *Leaving Las Vegas*. In the CD changer were several Smiths albums. Photo books filled with pictures of Anne when she was a child were scattered about her bedroom floor, along with her dark poetry, all hand-written, all concerning suicide.

Everything was in place.

With one last look at the corpse——*God, she had nice tits*——he walked out the door, euphoria tickling his heart.

#

Before moving on to a new hunting ground, Jake always went to one last meeting. There, he would pretend to be shocked upon hearing one of the group was dead, and then he would declare his fellow depressives faulty because of their inability to save one of their own kind. No one ever suspected a thing.

Not only was this duty essential, but it was a part of the pleasurable experience for him.

After the fun and games, he always joined a new group in another city. As he walked into the meeting room, housed in the basement of a Methodist church, he was surprised to find this new group bigger than any of the others, and most of them were women. Good-looking women. It never ceased to amaze him how many suicidal women were hot.

There were so many beauties, he spent most of his time with his legs crossed to hide his erection. It was very hard ——difficult, that is——to choose his target this time. After a month of deliberation, he decided on the girl that joined the group the very day he did: Mary.

#

*Yes*, she thought, *he's definitely checking me out*. Of course, he was looking at all the other women, too, but she could tell he was more interested in her. She noticed his eyes always rotating toward her general area, and when it was group feedback time, he always had something positive to say to her.

She mimed a yawn and stretched, pushing her full breasts against the thin fabric of her shirt. She wore no bra and smiled mentally as she watched him through stab-wound eyes. His own were glued to the shape of her nipples.

*Suicidal guys are so easy*, she thought, and she had a lot of experience, in that her favorite past-time was pretending to be depressed in order to lure real suicidal men into having sex with her. Afterward, she would manipulate them into taking their own lives. It was a hell of an interesting way to live. Mary was always traveling, and she always had plenty of fun.

All she had to do was wait until Jake asked her out, and then the party would begin anew.

#

Jake noticed that groups and the people in them were always the same, so getting used to the new set-up didn't take long. As usual, the guy in charge, Ted, was a former suicide attempt, and he had the scars on his wrists to prove it.

Jake's own story was the same, too; abusive/neglective parents, violently marginalized by other kids, dead brother, dead pets, rapist uncle, scarred biceps from cutting himself, social anxiety, etc. Not a single word was true (except for the scars; he needed physical evidence to show these people he was for real). In fact, his actual childhood memories were that of a normal, boring American family. Maybe that was why he did what he did; his whole life up until now had been a little too normal and a lot too boring. He liked telling these horror tales of his disturbing past, and after doing so over and over, he liked it so much it came natural to him. No one ever doubted his legitimacy.

Everyone else had pretty much the same story, except for Bill, who had tried to kill himself after losing both testicles and his penis to cancer. Jake found it difficult not to laugh when the poor bastard lamented about not being able to jerk off. Jake almost lost it when Bill confessed to the group in hushed tones that he sometimes got drunk and attached a strap-on to himself while gazing at his body in a full-length mirror. He also said that he felt the ghost of his genitals, as an amputee was sometimes haunted by a phantom itch, and sometimes, the strap-on was an adequate substitute. Then, Bill wept and everyone hugged him. When it was Jake's turn, he wondered what would happen if he kneed Bill between the legs. Would his astral balls feel the pain? Or would Bill collapse, crying and confused? Jake had to bite his cheeks to stop from giggling.

When the silly display was over, Jake decided he was going to ask Mary out.

#

As soon as she saw Jake approaching her, she knew from the look in his eyes that he was finally going to do it.

The session had just ended, and Mary thought it had been particularly entertaining. Bill's strange confession had made her day, and it was hard to contain her laughter at his brutal misfortune. When she hugged him, she was laughing, but she was able to make it sound like she was crying. She barely restrained the urge to caress Bill between the legs, just to see what it felt like and what his reaction would be. But no, this wasn't the time or the place. Maybe if it had only been the two of them, she would have.

And now, here was Jake, getting up the guts to ask her out. He watched his feet carefully, using his best shy-guy routine, as he said, "Hi Mary. How are you?"

Mary gave him her best smile. "I've been worse. You?"

"Same here." Still looking at his feet. "I was wondering, um, what are you . . . uh, doing tonight?"

"Not much. I think I'll just watch *The English Patient* and go to sleep. Why?"

Jake took a step back, his eyes now on *her* feet. "Oh, well, I just thought . . . I don't know, maybe . . . you'd like to join me for . . . uh, dinner." Now, he looked her in the eyes.

She twirled her hair around a finger. "I'd love to, Jake. Tonight?"

Jake mimed surprise. "If that's okay with you."

"Eight o'clock, then?"

Jake nodded eagerly. "I'll pick you up then. What's your address?"

She wrote it down for him and gave him her number. "In case you get lost."

They said their goodbyes.

As Mary walked away, she thought, *What a chump.*

As Jake walked away, clutching Mary's address, he thought, *Hook, line, and sinker.*

#

The Restaurant. Not too fancy, but not Wendy's, either. He ordered a T-bone steak. She had pasta.

As he cut the medium-rare meat, he toyed with the thought of sticking both fork and knife into her face and penetrating that soft, pretty flesh of hers. Obviously, there would be blood and screaming, but what would be her initial reaction? And how would the other diners take it? He envisioned her lungs filling with a quick breath of oxygen from the shock. That, in turn, would push her ribs and breasts out. Her soft lips would form an "O" shape, maybe out of ecstasy, probably out of pain. And the room would be filled with un-expecting gasps.

As she shoveled pasta into her mouth, she wondered what it would be like if she took the candle, encased in a colored glass globe, on the table and hurled it at his head. Would he duck quickly enough? If so, what would he say? She could hear the words tumbling from his mouth. *Please don't hurt me I love you I'm sorry for anything I did to upset you please tell me what I can do to make you love me again I'm sorry!* All right, so maybe he wouldn't bring love into it, but his reaction would certainly be sickeningly pathetic. Oh, and what an orgasmic experience it would be if he hadn't ducked out of the way. She could see the globe striking his skull and cracking it, or even better, it would shatter across his forehead and turn his lush, thick hair into a burning, raging halo.

#

"That was a lovely dinner," she said as he parked outside her apartment. "Thank you for everything."

"No problem," he said. "Would you . . . um . . . well, I was just wondering if—"

"Of course we could do it again," she said.

Jake's grin was big and stupid. "Really? Same time next week?"

"Definitely."

Jake bit his lower lip as he leaned his head toward hers, but she drew back. "Not yet. Maybe next week."

Jake nodded. These things took time. "Okay. I'll see you then."

"Goodnight, Jake."

"Goodnight."

#

Week Two: The Movie. The theater was pretty crowded, but the film, a romantic-action flick, was undeserving of the audience's attention.

Jake and Mary sat near the back, with a tub of popcorn in his lap. About halfway through the movie, he gained the courage to snake his arm around her shoulders. She did not resist.

As he watched the hero and the heroine kiss on screen, he got the urge to thrust Mary's head forward onto the seat in front of her. Again, he thought of blood, but he wondered if the seat had a hard enough surface to kill her, or if she'd live to have some kind of reaction. And if the reaction was loud, would the audience notice? Or would they attribute it to the movie?

As she grabbed a handful of popcorn, she wondered what Jake would do if she broke the hand that gently squeezed her right shoulder. She knew she could do it, as she had done it before, but what would his eyes look like when he discovered what had happened? Most importantly, what would he do? She imagined him painfully slipping onto the sticky floor of the theater and curling up in a fetal position. There he would bawl his eyes out in agony, and she would laugh.

#

"What did you think of the movie, Mary?"

"Well, it was good. I guess."

"Yeah, it sucked. I'm sorry I subjected you to it."

"It's okay. Thanks for bringing me."

Jake leaned his head toward hers, and again, she pulled back. He nodded. "Next week?"

"I'd love to."

"Goodnight, Mary."
"Goodnight."

#

Week Four: The First Kiss. They were parked in front of her apartment after a very expensive dinner. Mary said her usual thank-yous, and Jake started toward her lips for the fourth time. At long last, she allowed his mouth to touch hers.

As his tongue swabbed the inside of her mouth, he wondered what would happen if he gut-punched her at that very moment. Nothing fatal, just something to shock and confuse. Of course, she'd be pissed, but what would go through her head? He could almost hear the whispers of would-be thoughts skipping around her mind. Would she perhaps beg him for more?

As she playfully nipped at his lower lip, she wondered what would happen if she suddenly bit his nose as hard as she could. Would it be enough to sever his schnoz? Or would her teeth merely rip through the skin? What would he think? She imagined his frightened thoughts forming into desperately vulnerable tears. She heard him begging for mercy. *Not yet, Mary-dear. Almost, but not yet.*

#

They disengaged.
Jake licked his lips. "That was great."
She nodded, smiling. "We must do it again some time."

#

Week Ten: The First Hand-Job. They were parked near a forest preserve at night, due to Mary's request. First, she made him promise that they wouldn't go further than a hand-job, and then she caressed the lump between his legs. Before long, he was out and extended to his full seven inches. Her hand glided up and down as she watched it intently.

As he breathed heavily, eyes closed, he pondered the idea of stabbing her in the head with his car keys. Would she continue jerking him off for a few seconds, unaware? Or would her hand instantly tighten? She certainly wouldn't see it—-the attack—-coming, with the way she was enthralled by the sight of his sex.

As she watched her hand numbly moving along the length of his erection, she contemplated dropping her head into his lap and biting off his dick. Would it take him a moment to realize what had just happened? Or would he know immediately? Would he scream and clutch his bleeding groin? Or would he attack her? She would hope that he'd be too pathetic to attack her. This thought, creeping across her mind, made her sick, so she decided to end that particular daydream.

#

She wiped her hands with tissue from her purse.

He tucked himself away with a sigh. "That was wonderful. Absolutely wonderful."

She smiled. After a brief pause, she said, "I think we're ready for . . . it."

"You mean . . . ?"

She nodded.

"Now?"

"No, next week."

"I can hardly wait."

#

Week Eleven: The Night. As usual, they walked hand in hand toward the building where their group therapy was held every Saturday. Afterward, as per their plan, they would head to Mary's apartment for a quiet, candle-lit dinner before finally having sex.

After that, plans differed.

Jake had bought another copy of *Leaving Las Vegas*, along with Morrissey CD's and other assorted, depressing items, all of it double-bagged. After sex, he would tell her how horrible she was in bed, and that she could stand to lose some weight, and he was going to leave her because of her inadequacies, etc. These things and more never ceased to shock his victims. After that, he would improvise, using what he learned of her from therapy sessions as ammo. If she didn't seem suicidal then, he'd force her to kill herself.

Mary would tell him after sex that not only was he a lousy lay, but also that his penis was too small. She would mention any other physical flaws she might notice during the act. Then, she'd loudly lament the months she'd wasted on Jake, mention the scars on his wrists, then add that he should have cut down the insides of his forearms instead. She also had some improv ready, but if that failed to drive him to suicide, she would stab him wildly and later plead self-defense, claiming Jake had tried to rape her. She'd only had to resort to that kind of thing once before; the small dick line alone was usually enough to make her victims kill themselves.

#

Jake liked the nice dinner she'd cooked for them—a thick, rare steak that bled whenever he so much as touched it with the knife—but more importantly, the meal was quick. Both were eager to retire to her bedroom.

At first, Mary had wanted to do this at his place, since it would be much easier for him to kill himself in the comfort of his own home, but Jake's insistence provided her with a much-desired challenge, a little something to break the usual murderous monotony.

The act began like any good porno movie, with Mary

pulling Jake's pants down and stabbing his purple-headed hard-on into her mouth. Though it was an acrobatic feat, they managed to lie back on the bed and twist around into a 69 without disengaging from one another.

Before long, they were hip to hip, and neither one of them moved to turn out the lights. Jake had wanted to wear a condom, as that was what he usually did, but Mary told him she wouldn't do it unless it was the natural way. After all, she wanted his seed inside her in case she had to resort to the rape story, and since she couldn't have kids, this wouldn't be a problem.

Still, Jake wanted to leave as little evidence of himself as possible, so near the end, he pulled out and dropped his come on her belly, where it could easily be wiped off.

They fell side to side, breathing heavily, feeling the burn of physical exertion, but never looking at each other. After a moment of silence, Jake said, "I didn't expect you to look so . . . fat."

Mary's breath caught in her throat. This was something she hadn't expected. She spent hours a day looking at herself in the mirror, and there was no way in hell she was fat, not even overweight. Instead of the pleasurable anticipation of destroying another human being, she felt anger building up in her head. *Who the hell does this guy think he is?*

Mary did not respond, not even with a confused whimper, so Jake turned to look and see what was taking her so long. What he found in her eyes was something he'd never seen before, fury, and it was his turn to be bewildered, and perhaps to wonder if maybe he'd fucked up this time.

It was too late to turn back now; he had to plow onward or lose entirely.

"Maybe you should try Atkins for a while," he said. "It doesn't work forever, but if you did it for a little bit, you'd be able to keep your weight down long enough to adapt to a new lifestyle. You could be a supermodel, if you weren't so heavy, you know. And, well, your nose is kind of mousy. You'd probably need some plastic surgery. But, if you had that much money, you'd be able to get lipo, right?"

He watched her face turn red, and not in a good way. Usually, his victims' cheeks tinted out of embarrassment, but this one looked like she was about to explode with anger.

A corner of Mary's mind told her she should use the small-dick line now, but her vision was blinded with rage. This was no longer a game, and she was ready to break her rules. A hand slipped between the mattresses, seeking out her knife.

"Well," Jake said, "I gotta' piss. Maybe when I come back, we'll fuck again, but . . . let's try with the lights out this time, huh?"

Just as he turned to slip out of bed, Mary's knife flashed down and plunged into the bed where Jake's penis had been mere moments ago. When he heard the nails-on-a-blackboard sound of the blade scraping against the bedsprings, he whipped his head around to see what had happened.

This was the last thing he expected to see. In fact, he'd never predicted such an action from any of his victims. As Mary struggled to free the knife, Jake said, "You just tried to . . . ."

The knife jerked up, and she jumped forward, aiming for his throat.

"Whoa!" Jake yelped. He put his hand up to block the blow. Instead of carving out his Adam's apple, the blade struck the base of his palm at his wrist, and it didn't stop until it had opened his forearm all the way down to his elbow. Blood sprayed up like water from a lawn sprinkler, drenching Mary, the bed, and a good portion of the ceiling and walls.

It was no longer fun for Jake. All the rules of his game were blacked out of his mind with rage, and before she could pull back for another attack, he grabbed her wrist and savagely cranked it, breaking the bones of her arm so badly that the only thing holding her hand in place was her flesh and muscle.

The knife clinked to the floor, and though Mary's hand hung at a ninety degree angle from her arm, she did not scream. Jake wondered if she'd even felt it. At this point, Jake couldn't understand why Mary wasn't giving in like the others.

Mary couldn't figure out for the life of her why Jake was acting like this. Wasn't this the same pathetic loser who could barely maintain eye contact in their meetings?

The one thing both of them knew was one had to get to the knife before the other did. They lunged at the same time, and just like a cartoon, their heads connected, and both spilled backward, holding their temples. Blood got into Jake's eyes when he did this, and he roared as he tried to wipe them clean.

Because of his hesitation, Mary got the knife with her good hand, and she jabbed it down at Jake as hard as she could. This time, the blade parted his scalp, and the point made it through his skull, but it did not pierce his brain, as she had intended.

Before she could pull it out, he pushed her down and felt around his head for the knife. When he found the handle, he gritted his teeth and pulled it out, turning his head to the side so the blood wouldn't run down into his eyes again. He was feeling slightly dazed, but this helped keep the pain down to a dull throb, both at his head and arm.

Mary rolled off the bed and to her feet to defend herself, and when she saw the ruin that was once Jake, she couldn't believe it was the same guy who had looked down at his feet when he asked her out. It was only then that she realized the whole thing was a façade, and Jake was really someone else. But who was the real Jake?

As he advanced on her, she felt oddly aroused, as if she

could perhaps feel actual love for this secret Jake.

With the knife hand, he battered her arms down enough for the other hand to grab a handful of hair, pulling her close to him, while at the same time blocking his bare genitals with his thigh.

"You think you're going to cut my dick off, you bitch?!" he screamed. "You think you're going to take that away from me?!"

She yelled, raking her fingernails across his naked chest, opening trenches in his flesh that oozed red.

That was it. No more talk. Jake pushed her against the blood-soaked wall, and he thrust the knife against her tits, carving what he'd once kissed to scraps. Mary's hands flailed against him, but it was no good. He stabbed into her again and again, and when her torso was covered with red, drooling mouths, he moved to her face until there was no more resistance.

Still, he went on, sticking it in until he felt too tired to continue. He plopped down on her bed and looked at the annihilated clump of flesh that had once been Mary. *I beat you, you cunt,* he thought. He'd meant to say it aloud, but he simply didn't have the energy.

Finally, rational thought returned, and Jake realized how badly things had gone. Very briefly, he wondered how he could make this look like suicide, but common sense intervened and notified him that it would be impossible. Even if there was some way he could make it look like she'd done this to herself, there was a ton of his blood in this room, and his flesh and chest hair were under her fingernails.

The only way out was to flee. No, there wasn't enough time to go home and collect his belongings, he just had to go. Sure, they'd figure out it was him, and if they followed his back trail, they'd start to wonder about all those other dead chicks.

He stood to start getting dressed, but he swooned and fell back down. Where blood had once sprayed from his arm, it was now merely gushing in time with the waning beat of his heart. He tried to hold the flaps of his skin together, but there was no way that would stop the gore.

He needed a hospital.

But that would mean getting caught.

That would not do. He'd have to figure out a way to stop the blood. Duct tape came to mind, and he wondered if Mary had any in her apartment.

This time, he slid down to his hands and knees and began to crawl toward the kitchen, hoping to find a roll under the sink. He only made it a couple of yards when he slipped the rest of the way to the floor.

That was it, then. He wasn't going anywhere. Jake looked at his dissected forearm and almost laughed. It was how he'd encouraged so many women to do it. Not across the wrist, but down, and here he was, sliced the same way.

Every time he'd watched a victim die, there was some part of him that had wondered what it would feel like to do it to himself, and now he knew.

*The hell with it,* he thought, and with his other hand, he pushed his fingers into the wound until he could grip the vessels. As he pulled on them, he imagined he could feel the tug on his heart. There were still a few veins that weren't open, so he bit into them and hoped this would facilitate matters.

Now, the blood was down to a trickle, but he was still alive, and that made him impatient. Jake pulled at the ruined vessels as hard as he could, intending to rupture his heart, but he had so very little energy left.

The blood stopped, and Jake had enough time to realize that this was his last moment. He thought, *This'll make a kick-ass crime scene photo, one for the scrapbook*, and then he thought nothing.

# Family Man

A stiff wind blows chills through my tightening skin, and the ground crunches beneath my feet. Laughter drifts through the streets, and the sweet scent of candy tickles the inside of my nose.

A small hand slips into my own, and I look down to see Dracula. Underneath the make-up and blood, my son smiles up at me, showing off his plastic fangs. His fingers are cold and sticky, which means he's been sneaking into his trick-or-treat bag. I think I should say something, but the moment is too precious. Let his mother chide him later. Now is the time to enjoy the crisp autumn night.

My eyes meet with Suzette's over Duane's widow-peaked head. We rarely get to enjoy time together with our son these days because of work, and it's good to see her eyes bubbling over with joy. Perhaps it's the cool breeze that brings tears to her cheeks, but I doubt it.

We approach our house, and Duane stops to play with the skeleton in our front yard. The neighbors like our decorations. They believe we're in the spirit of the season. We win local awards on a yearly basis.

Suzette pauses to keep an eye on our son, probably because she has noticed his shiny fingertips, and I clomp up the porch steps, fiddling in my pocket for the keys.

The first thing I notice is the candy dish. It has been overturned, and there are no treats on the deck. The sign, "Help yourself! Happy Halloween!" remains, and I can see a tiny sneaker-print on it.

Then I see the door, and my guts freeze as if the frigid air has managed to penetrate my skin.

There is a bloody handprint on the door, and it shows only four fingers, and I know what has happened.

With a casual smile, I ease down the steps and approach Suzette. "Hey baby." I peck her on the cheek. "Why don't you take Duane to Mrs. Starkey's place for a while? You know how he likes her hot chocolate."

She glances sidelong at me. "Are you all right, Sid?"

I try not to look behind me at the door. "Sure. I'll call you in a bit, okay?"

This time, she kisses me on the cheek. I barely register it as she leads Duane away; I am too focused on the open door, on the crimson handprint.

When I'm sure Suzette and Duane are gone, I take the penknife from my pocket. The blade is not very long, but it is sharper than a box cutter.

Gingerly, I push the door all the way open, and I glance down at the carpet. There are spots of blood no larger than pinpricks. Anyone who isn't looking attention would miss them.

I touch a red dot, and my finger comes away smudged with red.

Fresh.

I follow the miniscule trail until I realize that it leads to the kitchen. Here, the drops are more plentiful. Just before I reach the threshold, I see long slashes of blood, as if something had been dragged through here.

I stoop down and peer into the kitchen at knee-height. It is probably an unnecessary precaution, but it always pays to be prepared.

"Brother Sid! Careful as ever, I see! What's up, man?"

I stand and step over the blood. The man in my kitchen is almost a reflection of myself. We are identical in all ways except two: he is more muscular than me, and he sports a mustache. My twin brother Stan believes this makes him look macho. I believe it makes him look like Groucho Marx, and judging from the rest of our family, my opinion is the more popular one.

"What are you doing here?" I ask.

He waves a dismissive hand at me. It is covered with blood and is missing its pinkie finger. A childhood accident. He shouldn't have been playing with Dad's favorite hunting knife.

"You could have called," I say.

"Sorry. This ain't the kind of thing you talk about over the phone."

"Are you in trouble?"

He shrugs. "In a way. Check it out."

Stan steps aside and gestures with his hand, a game-show host revealing a prize, at the kitchen table, where the corpse of a young woman rests, eviscerated.

"Why have you brought her here?" I ask.

"I need your help."

The answer is immediate, without consideration. "No."

"Come on, man! I need you back in the game!"

"You're on your own," I say. "Take this body out of here before my wife and son get home."

Stan's lower lip quivers. "I can't do this without you, bro. You were always the brains of the operation. I'm screwing everything up without you. This broad's the mayor's daughter, and I didn't figure that out until it was too late."

I sigh. "Why do you think I stopped working with you? You took too many chances. I can't bail you out of everything."

Stan grins, and the mustache slithers beneath his nose. "Bro, get real. The thrill comes from taking chances, not from being careful all the time. That's why I need you,

Sid. You're the yin to my yang. Together, we're like . . . like the dynamic duo, or something."

"I think <u>you</u> need to get real. Weren't you listening to anything Dad taught us? We have urges, Brother Stan, just like Dad and Grandpa. They always told us to be careful. Look what your thrills have gotten you." I point to the mayor's daughter.

Stan sniffs and wipes his nose with the back of his hand. I don't know if he is aware of doing this, but it is something he has always done when he wasn't getting his way.

"Dad always liked you best," he says.

"That's because I always listened to him when he was trying to teach us something," I say.

"I'm willing to learn now." He shows me his palms, both blood-red, as if he expects a hug. "Whatever you say, we'll do, Brother Sid. Deal?"

I shake my head. "I'm a family man now. I have to think of Suzette and Duane."

He smiles, but his teeth don't show. His head starts bobbing up and down, a nervous tick that Dad used to have when he was frustrated. "I knew you'd say that. How about this? If you don't partner up with me like in the old days, I'll kill your precious family." He produces a large hunting knife from behind the corpse. It is red, and it is Dad's. It's the same blade that took Stan's finger when we were kids.

"Come on, Brother Stan. You don't mean that."

"I do, Brother Sidney. I was at least paying attention to <u>one</u> of Dad's sermons. 'Always stick with your brother. No one else is going to understand what you need to do.' Remember?"

I do, but something tells me Dad never saw this moment coming. Anger burns the chilly night air from my skin, and I say, "What if *I* just kill *you*?"

Stan laughs. "You couldn't do that. You like me too much."

Which is true. The anger dissipates, and I look away from my twin brother's eyes.

I open my mouth to apologize when I hear a feminine voice say, "I would. I don't like you at all."

I look up from my feet, and there is Suzette, holding her own knife, which she has just drawn across Stan's throat. I had not heard her come in, and judging from Stan's wide eyes and open windpipe, he had not, either.

I'd taught her well.

Stan flails around for a while, but all he can breathe at this point is his own blood, so it doesn't take long for him to drop to the floor. Suzette steps around him and hugs me.

"I thought I told you to stop hanging out with your loser brother." She talks into my flannelled chest, so her words are muffled. But I've heard this before.

"I didn't invite him," I say. "He just stopped over, looking for help."

"I heard what he'd said about me and Duane."

I look at Stan's dribbling throat. "I kind of figured."

She pulls away, then stands on tip-toes to kiss me. "I'm sorry I killed your brother, Sid, but he was too dangerous."

I kiss her back. "I know."

"Mom! Dad! Look at me!"

We turn toward our son. Duane has cut his uncle's nose and mustache off, and he's taped them to his glasses as if it is a phony Groucho get-up. He waves his grandpa's knife around as he laughs. "I'm Uncle Stan!"

Suzette exchanges a glance with me, and I raise an eyebrow. The hint of a smile dances on her lips. We've taught Duane a lot, but he still has a long way to go.

"All right, kiddo," she says. "You've had enough fun for one night. It's bedtime. Take your uncle's face off."

"But Mom!"

She forces him upstairs, and I open his trick-or-treat bag next to the mayor's daughter on the kitchen table. A clump of body parts comes out, and I start counting the fingers, ears, eyeballs, and noses. When I'm done, Suzette walks in.

"Not a bad haul," I say.

Suzette ignores me. She looks at the two bodies and grimaces, her hands on her hips. "What are we going to do about this?"

I hug her from behind and kiss her on the neck. "Don't worry about it. I'm the brains of the operation."

# Pimp of the Living Dead (as Jack F. Graves)

It all started one Friday night as Jules Tarbell, III, fucked Mrs. Robinson, who had died of a stroke only the day before. She was already pretty stiff, so he'd had to spread a lot of K-Y on her crusty, cardboard pussy before sticking his dick in her. Doctor Adams knew this because Tarbell had paid him an extra three hundred to watch. Earlier in their dealings, Tarbell used to offer Adams five hundred to jerk off, too, but the doctor found this a bit too unprofessional.

Watching, on the other hand, was good for business. Some of his clients, like Pat Dickens, sometimes got out of hand and started pummeling the product. Since the dearly departed had to look good for their funerals, Adams had to restrict such beatings to the torso. Keeping an eye on his clients was a good way of making sure they played by the rules.

Adams gazed dispassionately as Tarbell shot his wad

on Mrs. Robinson's death-deflated tits and wiped his cock on her paunchy, wrinkled gut. Finally, he stood and staggered toward his clothes. As he pulled his pants up and cinched the belt around his slender waist, he said, "How was I?"

"Excellent, Mr. Tarbell," Adams said. His tone and posture never changed, and he never offered approval or condemnation.

"I want to talk to you," Tarbell said, looking up to the doctor as stabbed his arms through the sleeves of his shirt. Without buttoning it around his naked, glistening chest, he poked a cigarette into the corner of his mouth and pulled out a lighter shaped like a gun.

"Outside," Adams said in his even voice. "There's no smoking allowed in here."

Tarbell nodded. Once out on the porch, he pulled the trigger, and a smoking glow formed at the end of his Camel. Adams didn't say anything; he found things went much easier when his clients offered information of their own volition.

Tarbell exhaled a bluish-gray cloud. "My mother died yesterday. They're holding her in Chicago, but she was raised around here, you know? My father and his family are in St. Mary's, and she wanted to be with them. Can you take care of that for me?"

"Of course." Adams folded his hands in front of his belt buckle, as he always did when he talked business. "I'm very sorry. My condolences."

"Thanks." Tarbell took a deep drag as he gazed out into the parking lot behind Adams's funeral home. On the other side was a patch of woods so dark he couldn't see the backyard and house beyond it. That meant, of course, that no one on the other side could see them, either, which suited the doctor just fine.

"Where are they——" Adams began, but Tarbell cut him short.

"Mom and I were close."

"Of course." Adams nodded. "I remember when my own——"

"I want to fuck her."

After ten years of selling the sexual favors of the dead, Adams had never heard of such a proposition. At first it horrified him, and he was about to voice his concerns when he remembered that Tarbell was his number one customer. This was a business, after all; so what if a rich man wanted to fuck his mother's corpse? It wasn't like Adams was the epitome of morals. When the initial shock passed, he said, "This is a highly unusual request."

"I'm sure." Tarbell looked back to the doctor. "It'll cost more, is that it?"

"Um." Adams wondered what he should charge for this service, as it had never come up before.

"An extra thousand sound good?"

Adams nodded gravely. "Up front, naturally."

Tarbell smiled, showing off a perfect set of choppers. "Of course."

#

It wasn't hard to send for Tarbell's mother. The pathologist in the city was a colleague and a close friend of Adams. Not close enough to know about Adams's moonlighting job, of course, but close enough to cut through the red tape a bit quicker than normal. The corpse arrived within a day, not even touched by a coroner yet. She wasn't even embalmed.

The wake was scheduled for the following day, so Tarbell arrived that evening, checkbook in hand. Normally, Adams didn't accept such a traceable payment, but since Tarbell was also paying for funeral services, he thought it would be safe this one time. He'd taken the effort to fill out the paperwork before Tarbell's arrival, and he'd worked the extra money into the charges.

When he presented the invoice to Tarbell, the rich man

signed it as quickly as he could, almost as if he didn't even notice it was there. Adams thought that if he'd presented Tarbell with a form that legally bound him to allow a football team to savagely rape him, Tarbell would have signed it.

"Is she ready for me?" His client shifted his weight from one foot to the other like an eager child.

"Yes," Adams said. "She hasn't been embalmed yet, so the room might have an unpleasant odor."

"That's okay," Tarbell said. "I'll take her any way I can get her."

Adams forced a grimace from his face before it could appear. Such a lack of aesthetic taste displeased him, but he was a businessman, and this was his job. He swept open the door as if it was a curtain, and the bedroom beyond was a stage. Tarbell went in first, and Adams followed, his hands clasped in front of his belt buckle.

Tarbell took a couple of whiffs. "Can't smell a thing."

Adams thought it odd, but he forgot about the observation. There had been recorded cases when the decomposition process was arrested (one as close as Hillside a few decades ago). So what if old Mrs. Tarbell was such a case? All the better for Adams's client.

Tarbell licked his lips as he looked at the bed, where a sheet covered a lumpen figure. Adams had never seen him so jittery and excited, and he wondered if maybe this would be Tarbell's last time here. This was clearly something the rich man had considered for years, and if it turned out to live up to his expectations, would Adams ever be able to help him top this?

"Take it off her," Tarbell said, his voice slowly becoming husky.

Adams went to the covered body and slowly removed the sheet, as if it were a tarp hung gently over a car. It fell from the hook of her feet, and Mrs. Tarbell's pale corpse lay finally naked before her son.

Tarbell's breathing became ragged as his eyes glided

up and down her figure, taking in every wrinkle, every birthmark, every hair, every detail he could drink in. Adams carefully folded the sheet and set it aside before assuming the usual position. Without another word, he watched his client from a distance.

Tarbell approached his mother, first touching her cold foot, then bringing his hand up her thigh. His mouth hung open as he squeezed her flesh.

"She's still soft," he whispered. His hand eased up to her hip. Then, without looking up from his mother's body, he said, "You can't see anything from back there. Come closer."

Adams politely inched forward, not very interested, but willing to pretend. Tarbell grinned as his hand moved closer to his mother's breasts. At first, he paused, and instead of grabbing one, he let his fingers tickle her cleavage before coming to rest on her chin. He turned her head first one way, then the other, as he leaned forward until his lips were on hers. It was a chaste kiss.

His mouth moved lower, caressing the hollow of her deeply wrinkled throat. Down further. Finally, he touched her tits, almost weighing them in his hands.

"So pliant," he croaked. He kissed the blackened suns of her nipples.

With the gentleness of a doctor, Tarbell opened her legs and nearly gasped at the sight of her puckered and drooping vaginal lips. His palm cupped her crotch, and he massaged the flesh at first before dipping first one finger, than two, into his mother's pussy.

"Hm." For the first time, Adams thought his client was feeling something other than giddy pleasure. "It's warm in here."

Arrested decomposition was one thing, but warmth? "That's not possible." Adams reached forward to examine the body. Tarbell slapped his hand away.

"No way, Doc," he said. "She's mine." He moved his fingers back and forth and grimaced. "Ug. Too much like sandpaper."

He retrieved the tube of K-Y from his pocket and screwed off the top. Squeezed. Smeared some jelly on his fingers. Slicked up his mother's insides. He then dropped his pants, and Adams wasn't surprised to see a wagging wand of a hard-on. Tarbell was so aroused veins stood out sharply from his shaft, and his purple-headed glans bounced up against his stomach, making a sharp slapping sound whenever it came in contact with his belly button. There was a star of pre-cum shining from the slash of his dick hole.

Showing no self-consciousness, Tarbell spread more K-Y on the head of his cock before he knelt between his mother's legs. Gingerly, he touched his dick to the corpse's labia, but he paused before entering.

"Mom, I'm back," he said, and laughed. "Get it, Doc? I came out of her, now I'm cumming in her!"

Adams got it, all right. He smiled, but it was humorless. He watched as Tarbell plunged himself in. The doctor saw his client's body shiver, as if this was the greatest feeling he'd ever experienced. Tarbell's hands grasped his mother's breasts, using them like a mountaineer uses holds.

Much to Adams's surprise, Tarbell's thrusts slowed until he stopped. Had he come to orgasm so easily?

"Were her eyes always open?" Tarbell asked, puffing, out of breath.

"No," Adams said. "They open sometimes."

Tarbell shuddered and used his thumbs to roll her eyelids down. He continued pumping away, but this time, Adams watched as the corpse's eyes opened again. It wasn't quick, like a blink; it was slow, as if it were an actual struggle to get them open. This time, it was Adams who shuddered.

"Stop looking at me, Mommy!" Tarbell moved to close his mother's eyes again, this time only slowing his thrusts.

Her eyes popped open, and a gasp broke free from her throat. Adams would have thought this was merely the expulsion of gasses building up inside the corpse, but shortly after, *she inhaled.*

Tarbell screamed like a frightened child, and he pulled out of his mother, toppling to the floor. Adams started kneeling to help his client, but then, Mrs. Tarbell sat up, and she looked very cognizant. Tarbell shouted gibberish as her eyes narrowed on him.

She stood and staggered like a drunk. Bubbles gurgled in the corners of her mouth as saliva slipped down her chin. A noise came from her throat, and maybe it was speech, but neither Adams nor Tarbell could distinguish any words.

The logy veil over her eyes cleared suddenly, and she blinked, looking at her son. "Jules?" she croaked.

"Jesus fuck!" Tarbell screamed. He scooted back.

Adams could feel his heart pounding so hard his sternum hurt and his throat throbbed. He sank to his knees as he watched Mrs. Tarbell stagger toward her son, and it looked like she was saying something, but the sound of his pulse was too loud in his head.

He wondered how he'd fallen to his knees as he tried to force his body to stand once again. His legs did not respond, and it felt like he no longer lived inside of himself. He watched, almost disinterested, as his body fell forward. The world slanted with his descent, and he found himself looking up at everything from a disorienting *Twilight Zone*-type angle.

*Help*, he thought he'd said, but all he did was move his lips as the beat of his heart grew louder and louder until it drowned out all other sound.

There was nothing he could do as he watched Tarbell struggle to his feet. Adams couldn't believe what he was seeing, but not only was Tarbell's cock still hard, it was dribbling come. Had fear caused him to climax? Or did he find this somehow exciting?

Tarbell quickly answered this question as he picked up an easy chair, probably aided by the adrenaline that was no doubt coursing through his body, and threw it at the old woman. She didn't register its presence in the slightest, not until it made contact. It struck her so hard both she and it were thrown backwards, just past the bed, and against the window.

*Shit.* Again, Adams thought he'd spoken aloud, but he remained silent as he didn't hear the glass shatter. The chair was too big, so it thumped to the floor. Mrs. Tarbell's arms flailed as she went through the window, where she undoubtedly landed on the front lawn of his funeral parlor.

*It's over.* This he didn't even bother to try to say. He was too exhausted, and all he wanted to do was let his eyes close. It was too much effort to stay awake.

#

Tarbell's heart wasn't beating as hard as Adams's had been, but it still hurt him enough to make him unconsciously press his palm against his chest. He couldn't believe what he'd just seen, what he'd just *caused.* Had he really thrown a chair at his mother hard enough to make her crash through the window?

He rushed to the shattered glass and looked down. Not thinking, he put his hands on the sill, only to immediately yank them back. His palms burned where they'd been pierced by jagged glass. As quickly as he could, he yanked the shards free and cast them aside, shuddering at the mere thought of his parted skin, watching as blood oozed thickly from his lacerations.

This time, he was more careful, merely poking his head out and looking down. There his naked mother lay, crooked and puffy in the moonlight. Her eyes were open and empty, and blood gleamed all over her body, almost enough to cover her nudity.

"I am so fucked," he muttered to himself. He turned to Adams, only to find the doctor face down on the floor. The form didn't move, not even to breathe, and Tarbell knew he was alone in this.

He looked at his wounded hands and saw blood dripping all over the room. He saw red streaks on the window sill. He saw the broken glass he'd thrown aside had left crimson smears on the carpet. The final insult came when he saw his penis, now limp and drained, its tip shining with a bit of semen. It was on his legs in gooey strands and on the floor.

His DNA shone all over this room, and he knew from many TV shows that you could never clean it up efficiently. One way or the other, he was doomed. No amount of money was going to get him out of this one.

There was no way he was going to go to jail. Tarbell would sooner die, so without giving himself enough time to change his mind, he picked up the broken glass and unzipped his forearms from palm to elbow. The pain bit into him more than he'd expected, and he swooned. His sudden lack of coordination pitched him out the window and into his mother's loving embrace.

#

Doctor Adams's neighbors had heard the commotion, and they'd called the police. As soon as they found the Tarbells dead on the lawn, they called the paramedics and tried to contact the doctor. It wasn't until an hour later that they found him, too, although he wasn't quite as dead as Jules Tarbell had thought. They brought him to the hospital, where they managed to revive him.

Much to his dismay.

Shortly afterward, the police were able to piece everything together. Adams learned a lot about a disease known as catalepsy before he was found guilty and sentenced to enough time to be confident of never being free again.

The guards beat him at every opportunity, and the prisoners liked him, too, especially a bruiser with the lovely sobriquet of Nick the Dick, who had always fancied marrying a doctor.

# Corpusplasty

When I first saw the subject of the email, I wanted to delete it with the rest of the spam, but there was just something about it that intrigued me. "Tired of being a fat, ugly nothing?" Maybe I was crazy, but the line had a flash of refreshing honesty to it. So I opened it up and began to read.

"Going bald?"

I ran my hand over the top of my head, and I grimaced when it touched more smooth pate than silky hair.

"Too fat?"

My prodigious belly rested gurgling across my lap.

"Bad teeth?"

My teeth had never been straight, but in my old age, a lot of them had fallen out. I ran my tongue over the ones that remained and wished some of the gaps weren't there.

"Unsightly scars?"

My body was a road map of 'em. I couldn't stand to even see myself in the mirror.

"Penis too small?"

My guts stirred when I read this part. For such a large man, I was hung like a fly. I looked at the statue of David with envy.

"Just plain ugly?"

Oh yeah. No commentary needed here.

I continued to read: "If so, then we can help, and it's so inexpensive you'd be surprised. We specialize in what we like to call a Corpusplasty™, a complete surgical overhaul that will make you the envy of everyone in Hollywood and the world."

I licked my lips. Anyone who says he doesn't want to be beautiful is a liar. The idea of a Corpusplasty™ sounded so appetizing I started thinking about how I was going to finance this thing. Any plastic surgeon who had to fix me would have his work cut out for him, so I knew it wouldn't be cheap.

I needed more information; I scrolled down looking for someone to contact.

"Here at the Victor Frankenstein Institute, we pride ourselves on——"

I paused, and my heart tore at the insides of my chest like a hyena. After all these years, my creator had finally resurfaced. I'd given up on him, I'd stopped hating him for what he'd done to me, I'd even thought he was dead, and here he was, working as a plastic surgeon in Los Angeles?

It all came back. My insides raged, and my teeth ground so hard some of the molars cracked, and I could taste their dust on my tongue. I forced my fists open, distantly noting the bloody crescents in my palms, and I grabbed a pen and paper and took down his number. Before long, I was on the phone, and a chipper voice was saying, "Frankenstein Institute. How may we help you?"

I cleared my throat to get the growl out of my voice. "I'd like to make an appointment . . . ."

# A Place to Be

No matter how old Sam got, the thrill of feeling someone's jaw connect with his large, scarred knuckles never grew tiresome, and even though he claimed to most that age had mellowed him, there were very few events he considered to be more joyous than a good bar fight.

That night back in 2003 was his fiftieth birthday, and he thought he'd treat himself to a drink or twenty. In those days, he lived in his van, "seeing America," as he liked to say, although it was really just him driving from odd job to odd job. It was November, so harvest in Illinois was over, and he was trying to figure out what to do next. One thing he knew for sure was he was heading south, where it was warmer.

To celebrate his fiftieth year on earth, he found a bar in a dark, rural area that seemed rife with alcoholic possibilities. He had a pocketful of cash, and he intended to blow at least seventy bucks in this rundown, dirty neon tavern.

It was a place for farmers and bikers, and from the looks of them, Sam knew it was a local hang-out where home-towners looked askance upon strangers. He found a stool at the far end of the bar, away from everyone else, and started drinking. Occasionally, he felt several pairs of eyes burning into his back, and he thought a fight might be brewing. He didn't mind; Sam was almost eager for it.

After a while, he tensed up when he noticed someone was approaching him, and through the darkness, the fog of cigarette smoke, and the haze of his own buzz, Sam realized it was a woman, young and on the good-looking side. Maybe she wouldn't be modeling anytime soon, but he thought she was good enough for a lowlife like him.

"My name's Carnation," she said. "You look like a Mike to me. Or maybe a Sam."

"Damn, you're good," Sam said. "Right on the second try. We don't know each other, do we?"

"Nope," she said, "but what say we get to know each other. Buy me a beer, huh?"

Sam obliged, and with a grin. Fifty was old, but he'd aged well. Hard work had kept him fit, and poverty had kept him skinny. It helped that he still had a full, shaggy head of hair, and the grizzle at his temples added only sophistication to his gritty features. In short, pussy was not alien to him in the slightest, although it had been a while since his last taste; one month, was it? A farmer's wife. Her husband had a bad back and could no longer give it to her, so Sam was willing to help her out. He didn't usually sleep with married women, but she was too hot to go to waste. Thirty years old, real blonde, curves in the right places, which was rare in a farmer's wife.

The more Sam looked at Carnation, the more she reminded him of this last woman, but Carnation couldn't have been older than twenty-five.

Sam was bored with his life, so he asked about hers. She didn't get very far into her story; in fact, she didn't even get to say her last name, since a rather large man with the longest mullet known to science approached, and from the way he looked at Sam's hand on Carnation's ass, Sam guessed he was the girl's boyfriend.

"Just what do you think--?" Mullet started.

Carnation interrupted: "I'm not your woman, Zed, no matter how many times you ask me if I'd like to fuck. Why don't you go play with the other boys?"

Zed's face went through several shades before he rushed forward with a raised fist. At first, Sam thought this yokel was going to strike Carnation, but adrenaline quickly sobered him up just in time to block the blow meant for him, and he sent Zed away with several knuckles on his teeth.

Sam wasn't one for instigating violence. His time in Vietnam had cured him of his youthful urge to seek out trouble and thrash it within an inch of its life. However, if trouble came to *him*, he had no problem in dealing with it. In fact, he *liked* to deal with it, especially if it was a bar fight in the middle of nowhere, where you could settle disputes with very few consequences, as long as no one died. Police in these isolated towns were surprisingly understanding.

But most constables took offense to strangers, which was what Sam was, and he hoped nobody would be too put out by him knocking around what looked like the village idiot.

When Mullet Man straightened himself up, Sam could read on his face that he was getting ready to fire off another attempt. Sam jabbed his fist into Zed's jaw, hoping to turn off this young fool's aggression like it was a radio transmission.

Zed stumbled backward into a table, knocking it and two chairs over. A globe containing a lit candle rolled across the floor, snuffing itself when it landed upside down.

Much to Sam's chagrin, Zed did not stay down, and neither did his two friends. One was a skinny, balding guy with a wispy handlebar mustache, and the other was a fat dude with an atrocious mullet and a Skynyrd shirt. They were both ready to defend their fallen bro, even if it meant ganging up on a middle-aged man. Sam felt certain he could take the skinny guy, but the fat dude? That was up for debate. Maybe if they fought fair and came at him one at a time . . . .

Wishful thinking. They rushed him in unison, and Sam balled his fists tightly, ready to go down swinging. At the last second, he decided to aim his attempts at Skynyrd, whose weight marked him as a far more formidable opponent. Sam reared back and hit the fat bastard with his best haymaker. Skynyrd grunted and fell back, unconscious before he hit the ground.

Skinny managed to get a punch in, and he hit harder than Sam had expected. His head rocked back, and he would have dropped if not for the bar. As he tried to steady himself, Skinny stepped in with a jab to the kidneys, and Sam went to his knees.

"You son of a bitch!" Skinny roared.

The punk's bony hand grabbed a fistful of Sam's hair. He knew what was coming next, and while most would steel themselves for the inevitable pain of having one's face smashed into a bar, Sam reared his head back, taking Skinny by surprise, shocking him into releasing his grip on Sam's hair.

Sam threw an elbow into Skinny's crotch, and his target doubled over, clutching his genitals as he tried to breathe. The attempt was short-lived as Sam whirled and put his fist into Skinny's face, dropping him like a bag full of Jell-O.

"Holy shit!" crowed a voice which sounded oddly familiar to Sam, but he couldn't place it. He turned to see a man who looked to be about his age, and he was wearing an army coat. Sam knew this person, but he wasn't sure who he was. Maybe from the war?

He didn't have time to pursue this thought. Carnation stepped over Zed and kissed Sam full on the lips, tongue and all. It was a bit sudden for a woman he'd just met, but he liked the way she felt against his body, so he wrapped his hands in her hair and kissed back.

"That was awesome," she said, breathing heavily. "You whipped Zed's ass. No one's done that before. I like you."

"I agree," said Army Coat. "I ain't seen an ass-kickin' like that in years. How the hell are you, Sam?"

Sam blinked, forgetting about the gorgeous woman pressed against him, and he renewed his attempt at placing the stranger's face.

The man realized this, and he removed his baseball cap, revealing sparse hair and a gray scalp. Grinning, he said, "Don't you recognize me? It's Phil!"

The name came hurtling out of the past, and memory struck Sam harder than Zed ever could have. "Damn! Phil Genaro! It's been ages! What's happening?"

The two men came together in an embrace, slapping each other on the back. "Just trying to eke out a life," Phil said. "Last time I saw you was, what? The VA Hospital?"

Sam nodded, grimacing at the image of the last time he'd seen Phil, who'd been shot in the chest and was hooked up to all manner of tubes and machines. Sam hadn't been wounded, but he always made a point of visiting his hospitalized friends after the war was over and he'd been discharged. When his money ran out, he went home to see if he could get regular work. There wasn't a lot there, since his parents had sold the farm, and jobs were scarce, so he began wandering the country doing odd jobs.

The bartender broke him away from exploring these thoughts. "Hope you fellas're done reminiscing. I called the sheriff, and he should be here soon."

"Aw, come on, Chris," Phil said. "Cut him some slack. He's an old war buddy of mine."

"Started a fight in my bar."

"Zed started it," Phil said.

"Your buddy's dick started it."

"There's where I beg to differ," Sam said. "I was just minding my own—"

The door opened, and in stepped the beefiest man Sam had ever seen in a police uniform. A balding crew cut perched on his head like a dying crab on a rock, and his beady eyes peered out from a Pillsbury Doughboy face. Sam didn't think the sheriff could reach his gun under the hanging flab of his gut.

"Hey, Chris," the sheriff said with a slight rasp in his voice. "What's the trouble?" As if he didn't see the unconscious threesome.

"No trouble now." Chris wiped down the bar's surface. "Was a fight, though." He nodded to Sam.

"Come on," Phil said again. "This was nothing—"

The sheriff looked past him and Sam to Carnation. "How'd I know you'd be involved, darlin'?"

"I didn't do anything." Carnation stepped away from Sam and put her hands on her hips, which Sam noticed happily, were bare and beautiful.

"Zed prob'ly didn't think so," the sheriff said.

"Zed's an idiot." Carnation's face dared the sheriff to say otherwise.

"I saw the whole thing, Mark," Phil said, and he explained the situation. Sam added a comment every once in a while, which was usually met by a shut-yer-goddam-mouth glance from the sheriff, but Phil had most of it down pat.

The sheriff turned his gaze to Zed, Skinny, and Skynyrd, chewing the inside of his mouth. Finally, he looked at Sam. "I reckon if they press charges I'll have to find you. Otherwise, you're free to go."

"And you're free to get the hell out of my bar," Chris said casually. He poured a beer for a newcomer. "I don't want to see you here again."

Sam shrugged. "Fair enough."

For a moment, he toyed with the idea of leaving no tip, but he thought leaving a couple of pennies—-his two cents--would be more insulting. Chris palmed the change and gave Sam a dirty look. Sam pretended not to notice.

"I know another place we can go," Phil said. "One dollar PBR personal pitchers. That's thirty-two ounces for a buck, and that ain't bad."

"Sure," Sam said. He turned to Carnation. "Do you want to join us?"

Carnation looked down at Zed and grimaced. "Absolutely."

As Phil paid for his own drink, Sam started toward the door. The sheriff stepped in his path and poked a rigid finger into his chest, striking perfectly between the ribs.

"A word to the wise, buddy," the sheriff said. "Don't get in trouble around here. I don't like Zed and his crew, but I dislike strangers who start fights more, got me?"

Sam gritted his teeth. If it had been anyone else he would have broken that finger backward and punched him in the face. It was a cop, though, and Sam only nodded.

"Good. Now go. Remember what I said."

Outside, Sam said he would follow Phil's car, a battered VW Bug from decades ago, to the other bar, and Carnation hopped into Sam's rusty old van. She smiled when she saw the mattress on the floor in the back.

"Sleep here much?" she asked.

"Yeah." Sam stuck the key into the ignition. "I live in this van. It's not much, but it's comfortable."

"Take many women in here?"

Sam winked. "One or two."

She rooted around in her purse as Sam started following Phil. Carnation finally pulled out a pack of Newports and lit one up. "No job?" she asked, her words locked in exhaled smoke.

"Nothing regular," Sam said. "I work here and there. Mostly farming. That's what I'm best at."

"I'd say you're best at pounding the shit out of people who have it coming," she said with a crooked smile.

"That, too," Sam said without much mirth.

"You and Phil were in Vietnam, huh?"

Sam nodded, watching the road ahead of him.

"My dad died there. I never really knew him."

Silence.

"You don't like to talk about it."

"Not really."

Carnation looked like she wanted to say more, but they'd just turned into the parking lot of another bar, just behind Phil's Bug. There weren't a lot of spaces, so they parked side by side near the back, where part of a field had been covered over with gravel.

"Goddam, Sam," Phil said. He grinned and adjusted his baseball cap. "You're gonna' love this place."

They entered and were immersed in the sound of AC/DC blaring from the jukebox. Phil started bopping his head as he brought them to a table in the back, where he sat on one side and Sam and Carnation sat on the other. Despite the crowd, a waitress wearing a skirt short enough to show the top of her hose appeared almost immediately and took their order. Even more miraculously, it didn't take her more than five minutes to bring them their beer.

Sam looked at the thirty-two-ounce pitcher and was about to pour it into a pint glass when Phil said, "No, don't do that. These things don't pour very well. You'll wind up with most of your beer on the table."

"Okay, what do I do, then?" Sam asked.

"Observe." Phil put his hand through the handle and turned the pitcher so the spout was facing him. Then, he brought it to his mouth and began to drink. "Ahhh. I call it the mouth spout."

Sam nodded, smiled at Carnation, and followed Phil's instructions.

They drank and talked for hours, a little about what they'd been doing, but mostly about the war. Carnation stayed quiet while they reminisced. At first it was really interesting to her, as she'd been born shortly after the U.S. pulled out of Vietnam--and like most her age, she was enamored by time periods that weren't her own)--but since she was no longer the center of attention, she quickly grew bored. Finally, she leaned in to Sam and said, "It's getting late. I'm going to call a taxi and go home."

Sam, who'd been counting on pussy later, felt the immediate urge to convince her to stay, yet sitting across the table from him was an old friend he hadn't seen in decades. Getting laid was no problem for Sam; seeing Phil again might be a different story. Then, he wondered if maybe he could still have both.

"Why don't you stick with us?" he said. "Come closing time, I'll drive you home myself."

"You're a perfect gentleman," she said, "but it looks like the two of you have some catching up to do. I'll tell you what, though. Are you gonna' be in town a while?"

Sam shrugged. "I really don't know."

Carnation rummaged through her purse for a pen, and she grabbed Sam's hand. "If you're still around tomorrow night, give me a call." She wrote her number along his lifeline, but upside down so he would have to turn his hand at an unnatural angle to read it.

"I most surely will," Sam said. They kissed.

When she left, Phil whistled. "I just don't know how the hell you do it. Nothing's changed. You're still getting all the pussy in the world."

"I'm not complaining." Sam thought that he'd stay one more day if only so he could bed Carnation. He downed the rest of his pitcher and glanced around for the waitress.

"So," Phil said, "you've just been driving around, doing odd jobs?"

"Yep."

"Since the 'Seventies?" Phil's eyebrows went up, as if even his hair was struck dumb by the craziness of such a lifestyle.

Sam nodded. "That's right."

"That can't make a lot of money."

"Nope. Just enough to keep me alive and in relative comfort."

"Don't you sometimes just want to settle down?" Phil asked. "Don't you just want to find a place to . . . to *be*?"

Sam licked his teeth. Normally, he was about as maudlin as Jerry Lewis with his dick in a trash compactor, but now that he was buzzed on PBR, he felt the philosopher in him start to stir. "Of course, man. I just turned fifty. I'm too old to be doing this kind of thing. I should have the American dream right now. A wife, kids, everything. Sure, my life can be pretty exciting sometimes—"

"Like with Zed?"

Sam smiled. "Exactly. But there will come a day, and I'm sure it's in the not-too-distant future, that the Zeds of the world will finally knock me down for good. So yeah, I wish I could settle down, but in my own way. I wasn't cut out to be Mr. Suburbia, but I don't want to keep driving and plowing and harvesting for the rest of my life."

"I get it," Phil said. "What you really want is a place where you can sit on your porch and drink beer and look at the stars and think, 'This is my home. I earned it.'"

Sam sighed. "Damn, Phil, you must have put some thought into that speech. It was downright poetic."

"But true," Phil said.

"Maybe."

Phil downed about a quarter of his pitcher and wiped his mouth with his sleeve. "I think you should come home with me."

Sam laughed. "Putting the moves on me?"

Phil waved his hand. "No. I mean, I live in a place like that. Like I said, it's a place to be."

Sam, who had lived in many places and didn't consider any of them to be utopia, rolled his eyes and smirked. "Right."

"Seriously. If you don't believe me, I'll show you."

Sam started on his new personal pitcher. "If it's all the same to you, I think I'll just move on, come tomorrow. It's about to get cold in these parts, and I'd sooner be down south before it starts to snow."

Phil's face went blank. "Sam, if you leave and don't see the place where I live, it will be the worst mistake of your life."

Sam looked into Phil's face, and he knew his old friend was dead serious. He got a good look at Phil's eyes and saw that while he was indeed buzzed, he was not drunk enough to be melodramatic.

There was also a tiny part of him that wondered if maybe Phil was right. He'd run into one or two war buddies over the course of the years, and they had similar stories, but they usually tried to push their religion on him. Such proselytizers usually had the same wide eyes, and Phil lacked them.

"Okay," Sam said. "I'll check it out. But tomorrow morning. I'm starting to get a bit tipsy, and I don't think I'll be in the mood until then."

Phil smiled, and it was genuine, almost child-like. "That's okay. I swear to you, Sam, you're gonna' love it."

Sam drank again, and he was tempted to say, "I've heard it before, Phil." But his friend seemed too happy, so he only opened his mouth to drink.

#

*Thunk!* "Hey Sam! You in there?" *Thunk! Thunk! Thunk!*

Sam tasted old, wet rug in his mouth, and he wondered how much he'd drunk last night. He briefly considered going for the bottle of Jack he kept between the mattresses, to kill the taste, but he thought maybe it wouldn't be good to be driving with the reek of booze on his breath.

*Thunk! Thunk!* "Wake up, Sam! I know you're not that

hung over. You're still the same tough guy I knew in boot camp!"

Sam wished that were true, but as he sat up, he was grateful to find that the world didn't spin around him. It seemed he wasn't hurting as bad as he thought.

He slid the side door open to reveal a grinning Phil. He was dressed exactly as he'd been the previous evening. With his baseball cap on, he almost looked like he had back in the 'Seventies, but when he swept it off to scratch at his scalp, the image was dispelled.

"Come in," Sam said.

"Not till you at least put on some underwear," Phil said, laughing.

Sam looked down, surprised to see he was naked. He usually slept in boxers and a wife-beater. "Sorry," he said and quickly covered himself with his blanket.

Phil got in and sat on the floor. "Nice van. How'd you sleep?"

Sam shrugged and reached for a pack of cigarettes only to remember he'd quit smoking years ago. *I shouldn't have done that*, he thought as he went for the mini-fridge instead and grabbed a Coke. "Want one?"

"No thanks," Phil said. "I have my thermos in the car. You ready to see where I live?"

Sam had to suppress a sigh. He'd forgotten about that, but what the hell? It wasn't like he was in a hurry, and staying another day would give him an excuse to call Carnation.

"You bet," Sam said. "Lemme' get dressed."

"You wanna' ride with me? Or follow my Bug?"

Sam scratched at his forehead, then ruffled his hair until he looked like he'd been in a tornado. "I guess I'll ride with you."

"Sure thing," Phil said. "Come on."

Sam was surprised to find the interior of the Bug was the complete opposite of the exterior. Outside, the vehicle was spotted with rust, caked with mud, and sported several cracks in the windshield. Inside, however, it was immaculately kept. Sam wondered if maybe Phil hit the dash with Armor-All and vacuumed the rugs on a regular basis. He doubted the seats were this clean when the VW had come off the assembly line.

"How far is it?" Sam asked. He clicked his seat belt in place.

"Just a few miles," Phil said. When he turned the key in the ignition, the car started without a hitch.

After they'd gone a mile, Sam said, "This Bug runs like a dream. How'd you keep it going so well?"

"I was a mechanic when I got out of the VA," Phil said. He patted the wheel. "Now I have lots of time to care for my baby."

"You retired?" Sam asked, half-jokingly.

"Yes, actually," Phil said. "We all are, in my community."

Sam cast him a side-long glance. "You're not in a cult, are you? Like Waco?"

Phil laughed. "No, it's nothing like that. You'll see what I mean when we get there. And now that I've mentioned it . . . ."

He pointed to a large neon sign which might have been new in the 'Fifties. It said, "LECROIX'S BLACKHAWK CAMPING GROUND," and below this, in smaller letters, "Privately owned. Alcohol allowed."

When Phil turned in, Sam said, "You live in a camp ground?"

"You bet," Phil said, grinning.

"In a tent? Or a camper?"

"I live in one of those trailers."

As they rounded a bend in the dirt path, Sam saw a gathering of trailer homes. They passed a wooden sign that said, "This section is dedicated to the fighting men of America who battled at Normandy on D-Day, both casualties and survivors."

"Are there many signs like that?" Sam asked.

"A whole bunch. Some are dedicated to us. Some of the places we fought."

Sam didn't know how to take that. On one hand, he was grateful that someone cared. On the other, he wanted to put Vietnam far behind him, to make it a war another man fought, perhaps an older brother who'd told him stories about what happened In The Shit.

"We're all vets here," Phil said, "from all the American wars you can think of. Some secret ones, too." He waved to an old man tending a tiny garden in his front lawn, and the old man offered a stiff salute.

"How far back does this place go?" Sam asked.

"You mean, time-wise? Back to World War I. You know how a lot of us 'Nam vets started living in the wilderness? To escape from people and war?"

Sam nodded, thinking that wasn't very different from what he'd been doing these past few decades.

"Well, that's always been kind of a trend, it seems," Phil said. "That's what Nick LeCroix wanted to do when he came back from the war. Others wanted to drink and party, but LeCroix needed to escape. So, he b—er, well, he opened this place up and welcomed others of a like mind."

Sam didn't want to admit it, but he liked that idea. There was a certain kind of magic about it. He was never much of a romantic, but he felt something swell up inside of him, and he almost felt like crying.

"This is me over here." Phil nodded his head toward a trailer with a big American flag tacked in front of the place. There were a few other decorations, and one of them was a black and white POW/MIA poster next to the flag. "Nice, huh?"

"Yeah," Sam said.

"And then we let the campers stay over here. There's never many of them, but they all pay in advance, and it's enough to keep us afloat."

"You're <u>all</u> retired up here?" Sam asked.

"Yep."

"Campers can't pay for all this," Sam said. "I can't imagine what the property tax for a place like this is."

"That's the beauty of LeCroix's deal. This used to be an Indian reservation. When LeCroix bought the land from them, a few stayed on living here, so it's technically still a reservation."

"That can't be legal."

"It's a gray area," Phil said, "but no one's ever called us on it, and I doubt they ever will. Nobody much cares about this area, except for us."

"Until developers want to turn it into a mall," Sam said. "I'm sure when that happens, the IRS will rape you. And you'll take it. In case you haven't noticed, eminent domain seizures are getting shadier."

"Gee, thanks," Phil said. "Don't try to scare me or anything."

Sam shrugged. "I'm just saying, that's what I always see. I can't tell you how many farms I've seen give up the ghost to a bank, which in turn sold the land to developers."

"Do you think they'd do that to a reservation? Even if there's only a handful of Potawatomi still here?"

Sam tilted his hand back and forth. "Maybe. Maybe not."

Phil grunted. "Well, anyway. How does that trailer look?" He pointed to an older place, perhaps from the 'Eighties, with no decorations at all.

"Looks better than a lot of places I've lived in," Sam said.

"It's got plumbing, gas, and everything," Phil said. "The guy who used to live there died a few months ago. Vietnam vet. It's yours, if you want to stay with us."

Sam smirked. "Right. How much?"

"Free," Phil said. "Your dues were paid in 'Nam."

Sam grunted a short, ugly laugh. "Nothing's for free."

Phil smiled, but there was no camaraderie in it.

"You're right, Sam. Cost doesn't always mean money, though."

At first, Sam thought it was a cryptic slam to his skepticism, but then he figured Phil meant Vietnam again. "You got that right."

Phil parked next to the vacant trailer. "Come on. I'll give you the tour."

Half-smiling, Sam said, "Does it come furnished?"

"Why, soitenly," Phil said, waggling his eyebrows. "Even has a fridge."

They got out of the car and headed up the porch steps. The door was not locked.

"Safe neighborhood?" Sam asked.

"The safest in the world."

As soon as they were inside, Sam saw Phil wasn't lying. He went from room to room, grinning at the Formica table with matching chairs in the kitchenette, the TV and couch and lounger in the front room, and the bed and bookcases in the bedroom. The shelves were bare, and he couldn't help but wonder what the previous owner's taste had been.

He couldn't believe Phil was offering all this for free, but Sam felt something he hadn't anticipated: wonder, with a dash of contentment. Though he would never admit it, he felt like he was home. The cosmos had reached down from the unfathomable eons and touched his mind. *This is where I belong*, he thought. *After all these years of searching, this is it.*

"Well, what do you think?" Phil asked.

"I'll take it." No hesitation, just an answer.

Phil grinned. "I thought you would."

#

It surprised him how quickly he fit into life at LeCroix's Blackhawk Camping Ground. By the end of his first day, Sam had so many new friends he couldn't remember all their names. By the end of the week, he'd heard so many war stories he was thinking of writing a Stephen Ambrose kind of history book. The only duty they gave him was to collect money from campers. He found it very hard to believe how easy life here was turning out to be.

He was particularly fond of Carnation, even if she was a little young for him. What he thought would be a one-night stand was quickly metamorphosing, much to his surprise, into a serious relationship. After a week of living in the trailer, she was considering moving in with him. Sam had his doubts about marriage, but he was very comfortable living in sin. The idea put a smile on his face.

Aside from this, Sam thought there was no finer feeling in the world than to wake up in the morning and feel the gentle breeze of the woods coming through the window, trailed by the aroma of life and burnt out campfires. On several occasions, he went outside to have his first coffee on the porch only to find a couple of deer grazing on his lawn. No matter how much he liked this, Carnation got a much bigger kick out of it. She started photographing them and submitting the pictures to art journals.

Sam would never admit it to his fellow soldiers, but he had always envied the hippies, even when he served in Vietnam. He didn't always like their ideas--socialism turned him off quicker than the time it took John Wayne to punch a Commie's lights out--but he admired their natural, peaceful way of life. Maybe one's removal from society and its trappings was the only path to contentment, and Sam definitely felt content.

He knew such a utopia had to come with a price, and it took nearly a month of living in Paradise for Phil to come knocking at his door with the invoice.

"Hope you've enjoyed your time here," Phil said.

Sam, blissfully unaware of what was coming, could

only grin, letting all his doubts float away like balloons escaped from a child's grasp. "I'll be honest, Phil. I didn't expect much, but this place has been Heaven on earth for me. I can't remember ever being happier."

Phil nodded. "I'm sure Carnation has a hell of a lot to do with that."

Sam smiled and nodded.

"Speaking of Carnation, is she here?"

"No," Sam said. "She's in town with her mother."

"Good. Because I'm here to ask a question, and I'd rather it be between the two of us. It's a question about 'Nam. Do you mind?"

Sam bit his lower lip and grimaced, tempted to say yes. But this just wasn't anyone; he was a man who had fought with him in the bush. "I guess that's okay."

Phil squirmed a bit in his chair, as if he wasn't comfortable with this question, either. "Why did you go off to war?"

"That's easy," Sam said. He still sat tense with his fingers gripping the armrests, though. "I was drafted. I had to go."

"You could've run to Canada. Claim conscientious objector. Put a pencil through your eardrum. You didn't *have* to go, but you did. Why?"

Sam sighed. "I guess I bought the bullshit, too. That crap about how the best defense was a good offense. I thought America was next for the Commies, as soon as they had Vietnam in their grasp. The Domino Effect, I think it was called."

"Right!" Phil said, finally smiling. "Me, too!"

"Great, we're both idiots."

"Maybe for falling for such a lie," Phil said, "but not for wanting to defend our home. That's not just a noble undertaking, it's necessary."

"Okay," Sam said. "I don't know where you're going with this, but—"

"You agree though, right?" Phil asked. "That defending

your home is important?"

Sam, who had been traveling for most of his life with only a van as home, wouldn't have believed so a month ago, but now that he finally had a place to be, he thought Phil was right. Sam *would* defend LeCroix's Blackhawk Camping Ground with his life if need be.

"Of course," he said at last, "it's important."

"Good, because I lied to you about how LeCroix came upon this land, and it's vital that you know about this."

"It wasn't a reservation?" Sam asked.

"No, it *was*. And LeCroix *did* buy it from the Potawatomi, but you need to know how this came to be."

Sam shrugged. "Lay it on me. I've got all day."

Phil missed Sam's small attempt at humor and continued to plow on. "Well, Native Americans rarely want to leave their land, right? Us white folks have made them move so many times that when they find a place to be, they want to keep it. Well, this was the reservation given to them by the government back in the late 1800's, and they managed to stay here for many years, but by the time LeCroix came along, they *wanted* to leave. Why is that, do you think?"

"Some curse, no doubt," Sam said. Having read a good number of horror novels, this was mostly a joke, but Phil didn't seem fazed.

"Got it in one," Phil said. "A curse. And the chief let this land go for a song and a dance."

"All because the land was sour?" Sam rolled his eyes. "That's ridiculous, Phil. This is real life, not *Pet Cemetery.*"

"That's how LeCroix felt, too," Phil said. "He'd just come home from World War I, where he'd seen all kinds of horrors. Shit, Sam! The kinds of horrors <u>we</u> saw in 'Nam. The only scary monster he believed in was us, dig?"

"Very poetic, Phil."

Phil ignored him. "I know you're skeptical. <u>I</u> was

skeptical. But I know this story's true, and *you'll* believe, too. Soon."

"Right." Sam's hand went involuntarily to his shirt pocket, only to find nothing, reminding him that he'd quit smoking. "I like a good horror story. Continue." He rolled his hand.

"Anyway, LeCroix bought the land and lived in a cabin he'd built with his own two hands. Aside from other Indians, those who weren't scared, he was the only one who lived here. Now, I should mention that the chief didn't leave LeCroix out to dry. He warned him about the curse, that this land would be wonderful and peaceful except at the end of the year, when the tribe had to select their best warrior to battle with the spirit who lives here. If the warrior wins, the tribe is allowed to continue living here. If he loses, the tribe must leave or be destroyed."

Sam lolled his head back to look at the ceiling. "Come on, Phil. This is absurd."

"Again, that's what LeCroix thought, too. Very soon, he found out how wrong he was. The spirit came on schedule, and the remaining Indians made themselves scarce, hoping for LeCroix to prove himself a true warrior."

"Are you even listening to yourself?" Sam asked. "You sound like the archetypical wise man from the past telling the modern day hero of a horror novel the information he needs to defeat the evil monster."

"Would you please save the mockery for when I'm done?" Phil asked. "You might learn something interesting."

Sam rolled his flattened hand again.

"The spirit went directly to LeCroix and—"

"What did the spirit look like?" Sam asked, a slight smile on his face.

Phil just looked at him, pursing his lips.

"Sorry," Sam said. "Go on."

"Since LeCroix was the only one around, he had no

choice but to fight. Luckily, he hadn't been wounded in the war, and he was still in top physical shape. More importantly, they'd never fought before, so the spirit had no idea as to his style of hand-to-hand combat."

"So, he beat the spirit?" Sam asked.

"Like a goddam gong," Phil said, smiling. "And now that he believed the chief, he knew he had to stay in shape, and he also knew it would be good, considering the nature of the curse, to have others around him, since everything's supposed to be hunky-dory except that one time of the year."

"So the campground was born," Sam said.

"Not at first. In the beginning, he called up war buddies and invited them to live with him, thus starting this community. It was one of these guys who came up with the idea of turning this place into a campground. They named it Blackhawk in order to keep suspicious government employees from wondering whether or not it was still a reservation."

"Did the others believe the stuff about the spirit?"

"Not at first, but after they saw it for themselves, they became believers pretty quickly."

"Did they fight, too?"

"Oh, yes. LeCroix couldn't keep going forever. He died of a heart attack in the 'Forties. Luckily, there was a new crop of vets coming home, looking for a place to be. Someone from World War II took over, and so on through time."

"And you believe this stuff?"

"Beyond a shadow of a doubt," Phil said, nodding.

"I was wrong," Sam said. "This isn't absurd. It's crazy."

"I've seen the spirit with my own eyes," Phil said, his voice rising for the first time. "It's seven feet tall with three pairs of arms, except one set doesn't have hands. One arm shoots gooey projectiles, and the other's shaped like a knife. There are four legs with hooves, a barbed tail, and eyes on the front and back of its head. For a nose, it has a horn, and its teeth are like a shark's."

Sam searched his friend's face for a joke, but there was none to be found. True or false, Phil believed in this spirit wholeheartedly.

"I found this place while I was on a camping trip in the 'Eighties. I saw the signs about us vets, and I mentioned to the owner at the time that I'd served in 'Nam. He told me all about this place, and I knew this would be my new home. I'd just been divorced and thought it was perfect.

"The warrior back then was a guy named Mac. He'd been in 'Nam, too, and he was the toughest bastard I've ever known. I can't believe he's dead now."

"Died fighting the spirit?"

Phil looked at him as if Sam's face had popped off. "No. If he'd lost, we'd be living somewhere else. No, it was an aneurysm that got him. In case you haven't figured it out, he was living in this trailer. Died on your porch while drinking a beer and listening to a Cubs game on the radio." He hooked a thumb toward the door.

"So, who's the new warrior?" But Sam's stomach began to sink as he started wondering if maybe this story was true, and if so, why Phil was telling him all this.

"We don't have one," Phil said, "and it's almost time to fight. All our soldiers are old. I can't fight because of my war wound. If this Iraq deal was over, I'm sure we'd have some fresh blood, but we're all we have right now."

Sam swallowed, surprised to find his throat so dry he made a theatrical gulping sound. "And what does this have to do with me?"

Phil smiled, but there was no joy in it; it only widened his mouth. "I think you've figured it out, Sam. When I saw you in that bar, what, a month ago? I was shocked. Me, I'm just a scarecrow of what I was in 'Nam, but you look almost the same! Same build, same everything! And you wiped the walls with those assholes! You kick just as much ass now as you did when we were soldiers, maybe more! Looking at you, I knew you'd be the perfect warrior for us!"

Sam closed his eyes and chewed the inside of his cheek. "You can't be serious."

"Dead serious. We need you. Please, you have to believe us!"

"This is nuts, plain and simple."

"Fine, don't believe me. Wait until the end of the year. You'll see it, too! Just keep in shape, in case I'm not, you know, crazy."

"Oh, my God." Sam groaned, pressing his palms against his eyes. "Did I stumble like an idiot into the Twilight Zone? It looked like an ordinary day when I woke up. Or is this a dream? It's gotta' be."

"This is real, but don't take my word for it. Wait for the fight. You'll see it's real when you fight it."

"I can't fight something that doesn't exist." Sam dropped his hands into his lap. "I thought you said this place wasn't for weird cultists."

"We don't worship the bastard," Phil said, his voice high again. "It exists, we know this, and we annually kick its ass so we can live in peace for a year."

Sam smiled crookedly. "It must not be a good spirit, then, if it gets its ass kicked all the time."

"Oh, no. It's a scary bastard, and strong. But we're stronger. Our will is more powerful. At least, until this year, that is."

Sam shook his head. "I just can't believe this, Phil. I don't believe in spirits, gods, or monsters. When I was a kid, I was not afraid of the dark or beasts in my closet or under my bed."

"Let me put it this way." Phil clapped his palms together as if he were praying. "Let's say, for the sake of argument, that the spirit *does* exist. Would you fight it?"

"Absolutely. No question about it."

Phil smiled. "Good. Now, I bet you a bottle of Wild Turkey that it does exist, right?" He held out his hand to shake.

The look on his face was so earnest Sam couldn't help but smile back. "The 101 proof, not the 80?"

Phil nodded. "The 101."

Sam shook his hand. "You got a bet."

Phil stood. "You have to do me a favor, though."

"What's that?"

"Keep in shape," Phil said. "Maybe even train a little, okay?"

Sam didn't want to go down this path again, so to placate his friend, he said, "Sure thing, Phil."

"Because you're going to fight it."

"If it's real," Sam said.

Phil nodded. "You wanna' go to the bar tonight? Get some beer?"

Sam, grateful for the change in subject, nodded. "Let me call Carnation."

#

At first, Sam was tempted to ignore the whole thing, but after a week, he thought it might be smart to exercise. Even if he wasn't going to fight some monster, it was probably a good idea to not allow time to turn him into a fat slob. So, he did sit-ups, push-ups, and took up jogging again. On occasion, he practiced a few martial arts moves he remembered from when he was younger.

There were a few times when he wanted to tell Carnation about everything, but the more he contemplated it, the more he realized the only point of that would be to poke fun at Phil, and he didn't want to do that, even if his friend seemed to be a few rounds short of a clip.

The one thing he disliked about this situation more than anything else was how he was treated by his neighbors. Sam was no longer just one of the guys, a good fella to drink and laugh with; he was now the local warrior, the hero who would defend them from an ancient, multi-limbed, sharp-fanged monster. They treated him with so much reverence it made him sick.

It reminded him of when he was a teenager, just before the war. He'd never been one to enjoy church, but his old man made him go every Sunday. Back then, Sam had believed in God, but didn't think it necessary to go to a house of worship and ritual; faith was in his heart, and that should have been enough for the Lord.

The last day he ever went to church, he remembered watching the whole congregation—-including his own family—as they got down on their knees and tearfully prayed for the salvation of America. They begged Jesus to come down from Heaven and cure the United States of all its ills.

Sam didn't even cry. It was at this moment when he saw Christians for what they really were: a group of sad people looking for someone to magically appear and clean up the mess they'd made.

Much to his father's resentment, Sam never went to church again. A month later, when Sam turned eighteen and was drafted, his father said, sadly, "Do you see what happens when you scorn the Lord?"

Sam thought his neighbors resembled his former fellow church-goers, but he couldn't figure out why they needed this particular fantasy.

As the world grew colder and frost began to highlight the ground, Sam started wondering if maybe this was really some kind of hazing ritual, to see if he was stupid enough to fall for something so crazy. Or perhaps it was a joke, like a snipe hunt. More likely, he decided, it was both, and the "spirit" would be some guy dressed up as a monster, in which case he thought he'd give the trickster a hell of a two-fisted surprise.

Of course, Phil had to come up with a monkey wrench to throw into Sam's new conclusion. One day near the end of the year, Sam was sitting inside his trailer, wrapped in a blanket and drinking coffee as he watched the snow fall. Phil came tromping up the steps, and before long, he was sitting and drinking coffee, too.

"Beautiful, ain't it?" Phil watched the flakes melt against the warm glass.

Sam could only nod.

"The time for fighting's near," Phil said without looking at Sam. "You should choose your weapon."

"My weapon?" Sam asked. "Like, a knife?"

"Or a club. An axe. Whatever. Anything goes."

Shit. The spirit probably wouldn't be one of the guys in disguise. Unless the dummy had a death wish, of course.

"I can choose any weapon?" Sam asked.

"You bet," Phil said. "The spirit will throw its all at you, so you'd better choose wisely."

Sam nodded. "I'll think on it." Although he'd already made up his mind.

"Don't think too long. Next week is New Year's Eve, and that's when it comes."

As soon as Phil was gone, not just from the trailer but also from sight, Sam went out to his van and started rummaging through the boxes of his belongings until he found what he was looking for. Keeping it covered, he brought it inside and inspected it, hoping it would do the job.

Grinning to himself, Sam thought, *Anyone who tries to screw with me is going to get the scare of his life.*

It was December 30 when Phil visited him again and asked, "Did you pick a good weapon?"

Sam smiled. "This spirit of yours is going to be toast."

"Good. Tomorrow's the big day, and we're all counting on you."

"No worries," Sam said. "Don't plan on packing."

It was Phil's turn to smile. "Get plenty of rest. I'll see you tomorrow."

"Bring that bottle," Sam said, winking. "I want to meet the new year blitzed."

Sam expected his sleep to be nervous, even though he knew this whole thing had to be a hoax. He was tempted to have a few shots of whiskey or maybe even pop a few sleeping pills, but if he really had to fight, he wanted to be completely sharp. As it turned out, he was just fine without any aides; his sleep was restful and dreamless.

At noon, Phil came by Sam's trailer, accompanied by a handful of World War II and Korea vets, the leaders of their utopia. The current owner, an old codger who lost his arm at the Battle of the Bulge, knocked on the door.

Sam stepped out on his porch. "Afternoon, Mike. What can I do for you?"

"I just wanted to thank you in advance, in case you don't pull through. Win or lose, you fought for this country, and you'll fight for us. I thank you."

*Laying it on a little thick, aren't you?* Sam wanted to say, but instead he offered a salute. "No problem."

"Do you require anything from us?"

"I wouldn't mind a cheeseburger, if you guys're buying. I'm hungry as hell."

Much to Sam's surprise, they took his joke seriously, and before long, he was sitting at a bar with Mike on one side and Phil on the other. They were all eating cheeseburgers and drinking sundry beverages. No alcohol for Sam, though; sharpness was the name of the game.

Afterward, on the way back, Mike said, "The fight's at sundown, or rather just before. There's not a lot of ceremony, we just tell the spirit that you're our new champion, and the ass kickin' begins."

"I'll be ready," Sam said.

And he was, or so he thought. At about four o'clock, everyone approached his trailer. Sam sat on his porch, thinking he wouldn't mind a beer right now, and he remembered the Wild Turkey prize and rose to greet his guests with a grin.

"You ready?" Mike asked.

"I love a good fight," Sam said, "and I'm always

ready."

For the first time he noticed the forest was completely quiet. He looked to where he'd been watching a couple of sparrows earlier to see them sitting quietly, their song dead in their breast.

And then it came.

If it was a fake, it was a meticulous fake, the kind a Stan Winston or a Rick Baker would create. It towered over Sam, who was easily the tallest of his neighbors, and its six arms spanned enough space to hug a Cadillac completely around.

Looking into its eyes, Sam suddenly became very convinced that this was no joke; this monster was *real*.

Adrenaline pumped through his body, and the world went still. Mike said something to the spirit, but it sounded so distant Sam couldn't hear a word.

The thing advanced on him, and Sam felt suddenly reassured in his choice of weapon. He reached to the small of his back, to the gun he'd put in his waistband. His shock slowed him down, though, and when he pointed his old Army issue handgun, it was a dumb thing in his hand, incapable of the expected thunder and death.

Not that it mattered; one of the spirit's arms, with a hand shaped like a pipe, fired a gooey projectile which struck the gun from his stupid fingers.

It flexed all of its fists and showed all of its teeth as it approached, looming over him like a giant. Its shadow engulfed him, and all Sam could think was, *I'm fucked.*

It roared like a lion, and Sam expected harpies to fly from its mouth. His anus clenched when it reared its fists back for a multiple haymaker.

A voice muttered from somewhere, "Oh shit." It took Sam a moment to realize it was Phil, and his friend's voice was filled with so much dread and sorrow that it begged for Sam's painless death.

All it did was put steel back in Sam's muscles. So this thing was huge and had a bunch of extra limbs and all that. Sam had fought bigger guys who'd had better weapons at their disposal. Besides, he didn't think this creature had won *any* fights.

And it was wearing a loincloth, which could only mean one thing: it had privates to cover. Without a care as to how he'd look, he dropped to his back, managing to evade the creature's four fists. This confused the spirit, but only for a moment. It lifted a few of its hooves to stomp him, but this was Sam's moment of truth.

Sam rolled to his knees with all the agility he could muster and threw all his weight behind a haymaker of his own. He could feel the spirit's massive genitals against his knuckles, and it felt like he'd struck a couple of fist-sized testicles.

There was a moment when the only sound in the world was the whoosh of the spirit's breath, and then, just as it doubled over, Sam roared, throwing his other fist into the beast's chin, knocking it onto its back. Its limbs flailed, and the one shaped like a knife slashed into his face, tearing a bright, dripping gash from the top of his right cheekbone all the way down to his jaw line.

"Son of a bitch!" Sam jumped to his feet. Without hesitation, he began to stomp the spirit's head, beating its face until it looked like a rotting tomato.

"Yield!" it cried from its broken mouth. "I yield!"

Sam gave him another kick before he went to pick up his gun. He flicked the safety off, wiped some slush from the barrel, and pointed it at the spirit's eye.

"Don't!" Phil and Mike yelled in unison.

Sam sneered. "You're joking. I've only met this thing once, and I never want to see it again. This shit stops now."

"You don't understand!" Mike said. "If you kill the spirit, this place will die! By this creature's blessing alone do we live the free life we do!"

"Without it, we'll lose the land," Phil said.

Sam looked down at the spirit, who was trying to

regain its breath. Now that it had been dominated, the spirit looked rather pathetic, as if it was going to start crying at any minute.

"Let it go, Sam," Phil said. "We won. Just let it go."

Sam grimaced and flicked the safety back on. "Go on. Get out of my sight."

It laboriously got back up on its feet. "You are a worthy warrior. I hope to face you again next time."

Sam grinned, and for a moment, his mouth looked just as shark-like the spirit's. "No, you don't."

It bowed before it shuffled back to the trees and was gone.

Phil approached Sam cautiously, knowing from experience that a soldier had to come down from the kill-high before he was suitable for praise. When he saw Sam's breath evening out, he said, "You did great, Sam."

"Thank you, son," Mike said from behind Phil.

Sam's head snapped up, flicking blood from his slick wound, and for a moment they thought he was going to yell at them. He was silent for a second before he finally said, "Is anybody going to stitch me up?"

"Let's bring him to the hospital." Mike sifted through one pocket for his car keys.

"No," Sam said. "Phil was pretty good at stitching guys up in 'Nam. I want him to do it. And it's too goddam cold out here. Let's go inside. I could sure use a drink. And Carnation. If midnight comes and goes, and I don't see her, I might just cry in front of you folks, which would be the ugliest sight you've ever seen, I promise. Don't want to subject you to that, but I will if I have to."

For some reason, these demands struck one of Phil's heartstrings. His eyes began to water up as he thought about all those times they had wished to escape the harsh weather when they were in the bush, and could he even count the times he'd wished for a beer in the middle of a war zone?

"Not to worry, soldier." Phil clapped Sam on the back.

"Here, us old war dogs never go wanting. This is—"

"A place to be," Sam said. He smiled. "That's all I need to know."

# Shrink

"Just close your eyes and concentrate on your anger. Feel it burning in every inch of your body. Now imagine shrinking it down, bit by bit. Away from your fingers and toes. Up your arms and legs. That's it. Now compact it into a little ball and push it out from your chest. Reach your hands up. That's right. Hold your ball of anger. Now comes the easy part. Just push it away. Imagine it floating from you. Watch as it dissipates. And . . . open your eyes."

Chuck Wheaton cast his mind back to Art Nguyen's words and grimaced as he watched the thing throw his bathroom sink through the wall. If only that New Age bastard were here now. If only Art could see what he has caused.

#

It started about a year ago when Chuck saw a strange child run up to his five-year-old son and, without the slightest provocation, kick little Charlie in the groin and push him to the ground. The kid then loomed over his son and laughed as if they'd been playing an innocent game of tag.

Charlie merely whimpered.

The kid reared back, ready to deliver another blow, and Chuck leapt off his bench and jumped into the playground. The other children were quiet and watching, just like their parents, none of whom seemed concerned in the slightest.

Just as the kid's foot began its next sweep, Chuck grabbed his skinny arm and yanked the brat back. Stooping down so he could look the kid in the eyes, he shook the boy and yelled, "What the hell do you think you're doing?!"

On the woodchipped ground, Charlie finally sucked in enough air to begin crying. Part of Chuck wanted to drop the offender and comfort his son, but the stronger portion of him wanted answers. As far as he knew, this kid had never even seen Charlie before. There had been no altercation. If there was a reason for this to happen, it was locked in this wretched child's mind.

"What's wrong with you?! Why did you attack my son?!"

The boy's eyes were blank. He couldn't have been older than eight, and his chubby face was stationary. He found himself wondering if this kid was a serial killer in training.

"What are you doing to my son?" The voice was sharp and authoritative. It was a very familiar sound, as Chuck could hear it coming from his own mouth, too. An angry father.

As soon as the kid saw his dad, he began to bawl his eyes out. It was instantaneous, like flipping a switch. Chuck thought this was very creepy, but it wasn't enough to make him relinquish his grasp on the boy.

Chuck turned to see a skinny, balding man with the tiniest glasses he'd ever seen—-almost like a pince nez—-perched on his button of a nose. Though he didn't look very tough, anger boiled in his dark brown eyes, and if push came to shove, Chuck wasn't sure if he could take him.

"Did you see what your son did to mine?" Chuck asked, pulling the kid in front of him.

"He was only playing," the man said.

"Only playing?! Are you out of your fuckin' mind?! What game involves kicking people in the crotch and shoving them down?"

"They're just kids. You're a grown man, and you're shaking my son and yelling in his face! You should know better! You ought to be ashamed of yourself! Let go of him!"

Chuck knew this looked bad, but he also knew he was in the right. "No. Not until he apologizes to my son."

"You're being crazy!" The man stepped forward to grab his crying son's other arm. "You let him go, or I'll call the police!"

In retrospect, he thought he should have let go of the boy, and he didn't know which deadly sin--pride or wrath —-it was that made him resist this very rational idea, but he only released the man's child when the officer made him do it.

The cops believed him when he told them what had happened, but they didn't seem to care. If his wife hadn't been quick to bail him out, he would have been sent to county to await his child endangerment trial.

As soon as he was out, he decided he wanted to level charges against the boy who had hit his son. Rupert Schade, his lawyer, advised him against this. "The DA would see this as a desperate sign, and he'd murder us in court. You're going to have a difficult time as it is. Don't make this any harder."

But Chuck was adamant. If he was going to have his reputation unduly tarnished for doing the right thing, he wanted the kid—-whose name he now knew was Nicky Lorman—-to be punished, too.

Rupert had been right. Not only did the DA's assistant

use Chuck's plan against him, but the judge even dismissed the case he was trying to build against the Lormans.

As things started looking grim, Rupert begged Chuck to let him make a back room deal and end this trial before he found himself in a state penitentiary. Grudgingly, Chuck gave in.

Instead of going to prison, Chuck had to go to a shrink two times a week. While it was not his idea of a fun time, it was far better than the alternative.

Dr. Henry Forsythe was not a breath of fresh air. No, he was business-as-usual as far as the psychiatric field was concerned. He even gave Chuck a pillow to punch whenever he felt mad.

"I'm not an angry guy, Doc," Chuck said. "One questionable event does not make me a bad guy. I just did what any father would have done."

"Everyone's angry," Forsythe said. "It's just a matter of management. You have a problem, and I'm trying to help you fix it."

"You're the only thing making me angry," Chuck said.

The shrink shrugged. "See?"

But their time together did not blossom as well as the court had hoped. Since the results were less-than-satisfactory, Forsythe decided a change of tactics was necessary. He referred Chuck to Art Nguyen.

Art was a neo-hippie. Long hair, dull eyes, easy to laugh, not a hateful bone in his slightly effeminate body. He dressed in decorative robes and constantly wore sandals. The only thing he didn't do was smoke weed, at least not as far as Chuck knew.

Everyday, Art brought Chuck through the externalization exercise. Chuck had never felt like a bigger idiot. Still, Art was tenacious; he refused to let Chuck go after every session until he'd taken it seriously. By the end of each appointment, Chuck was good and angry, but oddly enough, when he earnestly followed

Art's instructions, he really did feel at peace with himself.

Of course, he'd never allow his New Age therapist to learn this.

After several months, he went back to court with a favorable psych evaluation, and he was allowed to stop going to Art. The externalization exercise was so effective, though, he decided to keep it in his life.

Every once in a while, something got to him. Bad. He'd feel the anger rising like bile in his throat, scorching the back of his neck. He would take a moment and feel the rage shrinking inside himself until he was able to push the ball-shaped wrath out of his chest. Inner peace always ensued.

And then a drunk driver killed his wife and crippled his son.

The soused bastard, Alan Burton, had no idea what he'd done. When he came back to himself, he refused to believe he'd done it. It had to have been some other guy who'd crossed the dotted line to crash head-on into the Wheatons' station wagon. When confronted with evidence, Burton refused to take the blame. He tried to tell them that Sandra Wheaton had been the drunk one. When this didn't work, he blamed Jack Daniel's. He blamed the bartender who should have stopped serving him. He blamed the cops who should have pulled him over.

And Chuck felt the anger boil under his skin.

Sandra was in the morgue. Charlie was in the hospital. And this mad alcoholic was mouthing off, trying to pass the buck.

Chuck breathed in, feeling his rage seethe over every inch of his hot, sweat-slicked body. He closed his eyes and imagined it as a red light twinkling with the occasional yellow sun.

*Shrink,* he thought, forcing the crimson glow inward until it became smaller and smaller. When it was the size of a baseball, he reached up to his chest and imagined pushing it out into his hands.

This time, the sensation was so realistic, he could feel his palms burning. Eager to be rid of it, if only to cool himself off, he pushed the ball away and tried to imagine it bursting apart into nothingness.

There was an explosion as soon as it was out of his hands. He screamed as he fell back to the floor. Flames licked at his body, and he dared not open his eyes. Crabwalking, he scuttered back so hard and fast that his head struck the wall, and he mercifully passed out.

#

When he came to, all was quiet. There was no sign of fire. Nothing was scorched, and there was no indication of an explosion. The house was, however, trashed as if the Tasmanian Devil himself had run amok here. The TV screen was shattered, the stereo had been reduced to jagged electronics, the couch and chair cushions were open and bleeding foam and stuffing, the lamps were in pieces, their shades torn to shreds. Even the carpet had been rended, and the curtains were rags.

Something popped and cracked upstairs, and Chuck knew that whoever had done this damage was still here. The guy was breaking things in his bedroom.

Like a sleepwalker, he shambled toward the stairs. It never occurred to him that he might need a weapon. In fact, he wasn't even the slightest bit angry. If anything, there was a twinge of fear, but for the most part he felt empty.

Once at the top, he moved past broken flower pots, shattered end tables, and shredded paintings, to his bedroom. The door was cracked in two and off its hinges, and as he walked in, something threw his computer monitor into the closet where it exploded and sizzled like a piece of meat on a grill.

Standing over the bed, ripping into the mattress and

pulling the springs out, was a man-shaped light. Red with yellow sparkles.

Chuck stood there dumbly, wondering what to do. Wondering if this was even happening.

"Hey," he said. "Stop that."

The thing whirled on him and emitted a bowel-loosening roar. Though it had no distinctive features, Chuck thought he'd seen jagged fangs sticking out of a slight indentation where a mouth should be.

He ran. Out of the room and down the stairs. He was about to go out the front door when he realized he had nowhere to go.

He turned and went to the kitchen, where he opened the fridge and retrieved a beer. He took it to the table, where he sat down and drank as he listened to the anger beast break things upstairs.

Was it possible that grief had driven him crazy? Chuck supposed so, but he didn't think this was the case. It felt too real. Of course, insane people didn't usually know they were insane, but still . . . .

He had to kill it. There was no other way.

Chuck went back upstairs and into the bedroom, where the beast was still destroying his things. That was all right; what he wanted was in the closet. He pushed the broken electronics aside and found the safe, which was hidden beneath several boxes of family photos and his wife's shoes. Four button-beeps later, and he was loading bullets into his .32 revolver.

When he emerged from the closet, the anger beast did not even acknowledge his presence. It did not turn away from ripping his night table to pieces, not even when he aimed the gun at its back.

He fired, and a tiny hole grew in the creature, all the way through. The bullet lodged itself in the plaster on the other side of the beast.

It roared, and this time Chuck *knew* it had teeth. It yanked the .32 from his hands and popped the barrel into its seemingly-ephemeral mouth. There was a crunching sound as it bit the short barrel off and crushed the rest in its bulbous fist.

But the hole remained.

I need to buy a bigger gun.

#

When the clerk told him there was a two-day waiting period, Chuck felt cold panic caress his insides. "Is there any kind of gun I can buy that I don't have to wait for?"

"I got some good pellet guns," Mel (according to his name plate) said.

"No, I need something with kick, like a shotgun."

Mel shrugged. "Two days."

He couldn't trust a hand-to-hand weapon. Nothing short of buckshot would do the trick. Chuck filled out the form.

When he returned home, he went to check on his beast, and though he thought it was his imagination, he saw the bullet hole in its back was smaller.

The next day, it had closed up entirely.

*Maybe I just have to make sure the hole is big enough*, he thought. *Buckshot should do 'er.*

Chuck rejoiced on the following day when the gun shop called to tell him the shotgun was in. He drove over as quickly as he could, picked up his purchase, and zipped back home. By this point, the house was trashed beyond all recognition. Nothing was intact except the building itself. Yet somehow the beast still found things to break. Junk littered the floor, and it was starting to pile up higher than his ankles.

The creature was in the bathroom stomping the toilet to a watery powder, and as the broken pipes puked up enough water to fill the room, Chuck could see the soap and several cans of deodorant and shaving cream float out into the hallway like boats over a waterfall.

He loaded the shotgun——grateful that he lived in unincorporated farmland, where no one could hear him so no one could call the cops--and didn't hesitate to let loose everything in one go. A cloud of shot filled the bathroom and tore into the beast, sending droplets of its essence in a spray, decorating the walls with wet splashes of red.

But some remained, and it oozed across the floor toward him.

So he reloaded and pulled the trigger again.

When there was no further movement from the beast's splattered form, he exited the room and slumped against the wall. He sank to the soggy floor and propped the shotgun next to him. His body was so tired he felt like a cornhusk in autumn, and his head fell into his hands. If he'd had the energy, he would have cried. For Charlie. For Sandra. For himself.

He didn't know how long he'd sat there, but the next thing he knew, something was moving next to him. There was a scrape as the shotgun was lifted away, its sight moving across the plaster wall.

Chuck looked up, expecting to see the beast, but instead he saw himself. His double's eyes glowed with the beast's colors, twin twinkling, crimson universes peering down at him, but the rest of it was him down to the scar on his chin from when he'd fallen off a skateboard when he was a kid.

It was holding the shotgun, but it was no longer breaking things. All it did was stare down at Chuck.

And then it handed him the gun.

Chuck took it, but he had no intention of using it. He didn't even think he could stand. There seemed to be nothing left of him except his body.

The doppelganger grinned, and it then put its fist through the wall. As soon as it made contact, it reverted to its fluid, gelatinous form, and it went back to its regularly scheduled destruction.

*That fuckin' Art Nguyen*, he thought, but it was with no

animosity. He felt nothing but resignation as he cursed the New Age therapist's name. If only that New Age bastard were here now. If only Art could see what he has caused.

Then it hit him: what if this wasn't the first time something like this had happened? If anyone in the world knew a solution to the problem, it would be Art.

Chuck pushed himself up, sending debris in all directions, and he pulled out his cell phone.

#

He met Art out on the porch. During their brief phone conversation, Chuck had told him nothing about the situation, as he feared it might not convince Art to come by. They sat on the steps as Chuck explained the problem, starting with his anger management sessions and ending with his double handing him the shotgun.

"That's it, Art," he said. "You probably don't believe me. Hell, I wouldn't believe me, but all you gotta' do is go inside my house. It's in there trying to tear out my water heater."

"I believe you," Art said calmly. "It's a rare occurrence, but I sometimes hear about something like this happening. Usually, it's caused by some kind of tragedy. In your case—"

"Sandra." Chuck closed his eyes and felt them burn under their lids.

"Yes. I've never had this happen to one of my clients before, but from my understanding, you're supposed to . . . well, sometimes we need to be angry. It's a human emotion. We should never be denied an emotion. The key is controlling yourself. Your anger was so powerful when Sandra died that it caused this thing to be born. But in the condition you're in, anger is necessary to your well-being. This is a time in which you *need* this emotion."

Chuck nodded. It all seemed too crazy to him, but then

again, so was an anger beast tearing his house apart. "What do I do about it?"

"Let it back inside yourself," Art said.

Chuck nearly gagged on his own saliva. "What? Are you sure? Because this thing is a nasty piece of work."

Art shrugged. "It's you."

"Okay, well, how?"

"I'm not sure," Art said, "but I have an idea."

#

Chuck cautiously moved down the rickety steps to the basement. His feet splashed through warm water, and he knew the beast had finally succeeded in destroying the water heater. It was now hard at work bashing the washing machine in.

He turned around to see if Art was still there. He was a few steps up, and he waved Chuck forward. Chuck obeyed, but as he stepped closer to the beast, he watched Art's face, waiting to see what would happen when the therapist got an eyeful of the thing. The thought had occurred to Chuck that this might all be in his head, and Art would be his reality barometer.

Art's face did not change expression, and Chuck wondered if maybe the beast really was a figment of his imagination. Then the New Age hippie said, "You never told me how pretty it is."

Chuck, who was too familiar with the havoc this creature was capable of, thought it was the ugliest thing he'd ever seen. Still, he approached the hulk of red and yellow, and though fear roiled in his guts, he started lifting his arms out to his sides as he drew nearer to the beast. As with the last few times he'd done this, it did not acknowledge him.

Chuck was a foot away from it, and he wondered what it would feel like. *Probably hot Jell-O*, he thought. His arms would most likely sink into the semi-solid substance, and from there, as Art said, it would be easy.

Chuck closed his eyes and placed his arms around the beast, holding it as tightly as he could. It boiled against his skin as he tried to fit it on his body like a glove. He could feel it seeping about his frame, creeping into his ears and mouth and belly button. The sensation was uncomfortable—-what he imagined drowning would be like--but it did not obstruct his breathing.

He imagined it attaching itself to him like a second skin, and he could feel it passing through his flesh as if by osmosis. Then he concentrated on the image of it coating his insides, and . . . he felt slightly slick, as if he'd been swimming in sewage, but there was nothing around him anymore.

"Congratulations," Art said. "You did it. The anger's back inside where it belongs."

Chuck spun and swung a fist at him as hard as he could. Art was not expecting it, so he took it square on the nose. There was so much force behind the blow that it rocked the therapist's head back hard enough to snap his spine. Art dropped face-down into the water on the floor, where he would expire from drowning fifteen minutes later.

Not that Chuck cared. By the time Art Nguyen was dead, Chuck had gone upstairs to pick up his shotgun, and then he was out to his car. He knew where Alan Burton lived, and he was halfway to his destination by the time Art gave up the ghost.

#

The clock said it was four pm, not that Charlie could see it. He was in a coma, and according to the doctors, there was nothing anyone could do about it.

He didn't see his father walk in and slump into a chair next to his bed. He didn't feel it when his father gently took his tiny hand into two bigger ones. He didn't smell the acrid odor of gunsmoke clinging to his father's clothes. He didn't hear it when his father started to cry.

If Charlie had been awake, he would have seen the blood dotting his father's face like chicken pox. It was all over the rest of him, too. But as grim as Chuck Wheaton seemed, there was a hell of a shiny smile on his face, the finest he'd ever worn.

# Timely

Damn.

Lights flashed from Peter's rearview mirror. He didn't need to look down to know he'd been zipping along well over the speed limit. A promotion awaited him in the city.

An impulse——very brief, but still there——made him not want to not stop. The county line was up ahead about a mile. A county cop wouldn't be able to follow him.

Why bother racking up another charge? Paying a speeding ticket by mail was a cinch, but fleeing the police? He would have to go to court for that one, and who had the time for that kind of hassle?

With a sigh, he eased his foot on the brake and pulled over to the side of the road. The cop car stopped behind him, and the door-mounted light blazed to life, aimed at Peter's side mirror so the reflection would nail him in the eyes. The sun still shone, though; things could have been worse.

Peter retrieved his license from his wallet and his insurance card from his glove compartment, intent on making this go as quickly as possible. His promotion to senior accounting manager depended on it. Ten wasted minutes might be enough to torpedo this thing.

The cop knocked on the window, which Peter then rolled down. There was a Smokey Bear hat perched on the trooper's head. *Good thing I didn't punch it.*

"Good afternoon, officer," Peter said, offering his identification.

The officer watched for a moment, his eyes hidden behind mirrored sunglasses; twin reflections, twisted and wavy, gleamed at Peter, and they looked composed enough. Good.

"Afternoon," the officer finally said. He took both cards. Without checking either one, he said, "Do you know how fast you were going?"

"Yes, sir, I'm sorry, but I was in a hurry." Peter had heard somewhere, probably on the radio, that honesty was the best policy in situations like this one, that when people told the truth, the police usually let them off with a warning. *Just give me a warning, please, please, please.*

"That doesn't justify going eighty-seven in a fifty-five zone," the officer said. "Wait here a moment."

Peter gritted his teeth as he watched the cop, in the rearview mirror, strut back to his cruiser. *Son of a bitch is going to write me up, and he's probably going to take his time, just to spite me.*

Peter closed his eyes and rubbed the bridge of his nose. Maybe if he drove super fast as soon as this jag-off was done, he might still make it in time.

"Come on." Peter tapped his feet and fingers. "Let's go." The clock said he'd been there only two minutes, but it seemed to have been much longer. The skin at the back of his ears tingled coldly, and butterflies swirled in his belly. The pizza he'd eaten for lunch started burning his esophagus, and he rubbed at his chest. He swallowed, hoping to kill the sensation.

Seven minutes later, the cruiser's door opened, and the cop got out, leisurely approaching Peter's car.

"Finally," Peter said. He looked at the clock. *This is*

*still do-able. I think.*

When he looked back up, he expected the cop to be out at his window, but no one was there. The cop was nowhere to be found, not even in his cruiser.

It then occurred to Peter that this cop might be so spiteful that he'd stop to take a leak by the side of the road. Peter cast his glance to the guard rail. Nothing.

Peter rolled down his window and poked his head out. "Hello? Officer?"

No answer. Peter's driver's license and insurance card rested on the blacktop, the only sign a policeman had ever existed.

He looked both ways before opening the door and getting out. "Hello?" Only an echo replied.

He approached his license and almost bent down to pick everything up when he thought the cop might be hiding behind the cruiser, and as soon as he stooped down, the cop would jump out and yell, "Boo!" Irrational? Of course, but the situation had become too surreal for Peter's sporting blood.

Without taking his eyes from the trunk of the cruiser, he bent down and scraped his fingernails across the pavement as he picked up both cards. He straightened up and waited to see if the cop would reappear.

*One more time.* "Hello?"

When the cop did not respond, Peter shrugged and counted his blessings. He got back in his car and started gingerly pulling away. His eyes never left the rearview mirror.

All he saw was the cruiser, lights still flashing, but alone, empty, almost like a corpse.

As it fell further behind, Peter's courage built up, and before long, the speedometer said ninety-five miles per hour. No one impeded his progress, and it was a good feeling.

#

He didn't think of the cop again until much later, at the accountant's convention. Peter, a featured speaker, had barely made it on time, but he couldn't help shaking his head in aggravation when he saw his place on the schedule: two hours from the moment he'd arrived.

*That bastard could have taken all the time he wanted to write me up, and I would have still made it.* And then he remembered the cop's disappearance. He wondered whatever happened to the state trooper, but the quandary did not last long. By the time he took to the stage, he only had his job on his mind, nothing else.

#

"You're falling behind in your work, Pete. I can't afford to have a goldbricker in an important position like senior accounting manager, comprende? The I.R.S. is auditing us, and I don't want there to be any surprises. Your report was due two days ago."

Peter grimaced. He wasn't normally late with paperwork, but the divorce practically lived in the front of his mind, and his wife wanted joint custody of their daughter. As if he had the time to take care of a five-year-old kid. He only got married because he thought that was what men did, and he gave Gwen a child because that was what was supposed to follow. You went to school, you got a good job, you got a wife, a house, a kid, and a pension, and then you died.

He could do without his wife, and more importantly, he wanted freedom from parenthood. He couldn't find a replacement family if he had to drag his kid around with him half the time. Taking care of kids? Wife's work. Pure and simple.

"Peter? You listening?"

Peter snapped back to attention. Chuck's customarily ugly mug was even uglier than usual; his pasty face turned red from the bald dome of his head to the dimple in his chin. His nostrils opened and hair pushed its way out; his jowls jiggled. If sweaty old nitroglycerin were a person, it would be Chuck.

"Of course," Peter lied. "Look, it's just—-"

"Your divorce, I know. I've been cutting you slack, but it's got to stop. If you don't pull yourself together, I'm going—-"

*I know*, Peter thought. *God, I know!*

He looked at his desk clock. An hour before the close-of-business. Chuck needed to go away. He had to be tired of fuming.

It took Peter a moment to realize that blissful silence held dominion over his office. He looked up to see nothing in his supervisor's place; Chuck no longer leaned on his desk like an overbearing gargoyle. The man had been fiddling with a knick-knack found on Peter's desk —-a tiny sombrero his daughter had made in art class-- but now it rested on the floor.

His gaze went back to the clock. Had he tuned out so badly that he'd lost track of not only Chuck, but also time?

Four o'clock.

*Forget it. This is a good thing.*

He went back to work on his tardy report.

Ten minutes later, Kevin poked his head into Peter's office, knocking twice on the open door. "Hey Pete, you seen Chuck?"

Something tickled Peter's brain stem. "Uh, he was here a few minutes ago, but he left. Didn't say where he was going."

Kevin shrugged. "Okay. Thanks."

#

When Peter came in to work the next day, Kevin approached him and said, without greeting, "Have you seen Chuck?"

Peter shook his head. "Sorry."

"He didn't show up this morning. I had HR do some checking, and it looks like he didn't even punch out yesterday. Did he say anything to you when you saw him?"

"Nope."

"Hm. He's never late, and if he can't make it, he calls in. Well, if you hear anything, let me know."

"Will do."

Over the course of the next week, Peter had this very same conversation with Kevin every morning, but after that, they gave up the ritual.

#

"Your lawyer called my lawyer today, and I can't believe what he said!" Gwen yelled. "How could you? What's wrong with you? Are you seriously going to say that in court? Are you?"

Peter didn't know what she was screeching about, considering all the terrible things he'd said to his lawyer, but the sound coming from her yammering mouth gave him a headache.

*Wish her away.* The thought came unbidden, and its stealth surprised him with an idea he had been tinkering with in the back of his mind ever since Chuck's disappearance. Rationality stood in the way of accepting such a fantastical notion, but what if . . . ?

But something in the back of his mind halted this line of thinking. He suddenly found himself wondering where the cop had gone. Was he hanging out with Chuck in some mystical la-la land? Or Hell? Or non-existence? Or could it be just his stupid imagination?

He gave up trying to figure it out. Peter had once loved this raving woman, but now the very sound of her voice stabbed like an ice pick in his ear.

As she continued her verbal attack, Peter scrunched his eyes shut and wished with all his heart that she would go away. Her voice didn't fade or come to a halt, and when he opened his eyes, nothing had changed.

*Should have known.* He looked at his watch. *Stop talking. I have things I have to do, and I don't have time to argue with you.*

When he looked up from his wrist, steeling himself for another half-hour--at least!--of nattering, his wife was gone. Gwen had been wagging a pen at him, and he watched as it dropped to the floor. The carpet held the shape of her feet for a moment, and then even that faded.

"She's . . . ." Then he looked at his watch and made the final connection: during each instance, he'd looked at a clock first and had been thinking of something more important to do. He'd simply not had the patience to deal with the missing people, so time had removed them from the continuum.

To where? Peter didn't know, and he didn't care.

But with his wife gone, who would watch after Carly, their daughter? Peter certainly couldn't do it. Where would he find the time? His parents were dead, and he couldn't afford to pay a nanny . . . .

"Carly!" he called out. "Come here a minute! Daddy wants to talk to you!"

He looked at the wall clock before he even heard his daughter's approach.

#

Peter expected questions, and the police did not disappoint him. For a brief period of time, the law considered him to be a "person of interest" in the possible murder of his family. Without bodies, he could not be arrested, so nothing could ever be proved despite arguments from his insistent in-laws. They managed to keep the case open with their complaints, but nothing ever came of this exercise in futility. A few detectives even tried to connect Chuck's disappearance with that of Peter's family, but once again, lack of evidence prevented any measures from being taken.

Things got a bit iffy when a local cop introduced him to a state trooper, who had brought a DVD from a missing officer's cruiser cam. The film showcased Peter's license plate very clearly, but a mere glance at his watch dispatched these two prying men quite efficiently.

Peter didn't make a habit out of making people vanish, but every once in a while, necessity prevailed. Gwen's father kept harassing him over the phone, taking up valuable time, so he made the old man go away. Occasionally, during a late-night drinking session with the guys from the office, someone would put the moves on a woman Peter wanted, so the interloper would mysteriously vanish.

Once, when a manager at the office wrote a memo entitled "Getting Started: So You Want to Become More Time Efficient," Peter found it kind of funny. Why waste time reading a document which advised employees how to not waste time? So, Peter got rid of the manager.

One day, the power went out, so his alarm clock didn't wake him up. When he groggily noticed all the sunshine in his bedroom, he swept up his watch to discover he had a half an hour to make it in to work. Just enough time to get dressed and leave.

But the rumble in his guts signaled not only the need to go to the bathroom, but also the need for sustenance. A quick rub across his stubbly cheeks told him he also needed to shave.

*Do I have the time?* He stared at his watch. *There's no way. But I can't be late.*

The hunger suddenly disappeared. So did the urge to defecate. A quick touch of his cheek revealed nothing but smooth skin.

*That settles that, then.* He stood and went for the

customary butt scratch, an unconscious action, but this time, his fingers found something different.

His ass was sealed shut. When he ran for the bathroom to look in the mirror, his underpants clung flatly to his front.

Frantically, he pulled the waistband of his boxers away from his lower belly. The frank had vanished, but the beans remained.

A scream rose in his throat, but as he looked at the empty spot just above his scrotum, he realized that this new development had its advantages. He could use the time he would have wasted in the bathroom in a much better fashion. And since he didn't need to eat, he didn't need to take a lunch break anymore. He smiled as he thought of all the ways he would spend his newfound time.

One problem remained: he looked at his clock and wished away the beans. He didn't want to have to worry about spending time in clubs and bars, trying to get a new wife.

#

Without these primitive needs getting in his way, Peter became a lot more time efficient. He began to win awards at work, and he graduated to sales. Not long after, he made it to the top of the department. He wheeled and dealed until the CEO noticed him. Peter made junior vice president before the end of the fiscal year.

A month after this, he found himself stuck at a railroad crossing, watching as a freight train chugged its leisurely way across the street. Looking at the clock in his brand new Lexus, he knew he'd never make it on time. Granted, his powerful position meant he could afford to be late, but he wanted the senior VP position, and anything short of punctuality would reflect poorly on him.

*Why are there still trains?* His teeth ground together,

and the all-familiar cold at the back of his ears burned away. *This is the Twenty-First Century. Why don't we have teleportation technology?*

He wanted to wish the train away when he considered all the time wasted in this car while driving to work every day. If he could teleport to work instead of languishing in traffic, cursing the guy in front of him, he'd have plenty of extra time to do important things, like work.

The train didn't need to go, and neither did the traffic. The cumbersome human body prevented things from being done in a timely fashion.

As the train rumbled by, he looked at the dashboard clock. Such a precision disappearance would be difficult, but . . . .

He blinked, yet didn't. Couldn't. There were no lids to close.

Hands no longer graced the steering wheel. No feet on the brakes. No butt in the bucket seat. The safety belt rested on the seat behind him. The sunglasses he'd been wearing tumbled to the floor.

Consciousness came unfettered from a physical form, yet somehow, all five of his senses flared, showing him more of the world than he'd ever experienced. Without giving the car any consideration, he soared through the roof, over the train, and as he passed along the expressway below, he watched as those stuck in traffic plodded along, even slower than the train in town had been.

His consciousness shot across the world without thought as to destination. Fate, or Whatever, flung him into his office, where he had the sensation of settling into his leather chair.

Peter looked at the clock. Plenty of time.

He reached for the papers on his desk and then remembered he had no hands. Only then did he understand what he'd done.

And Peter laughed for the first time in his life.

# Baseball Players are a Superstitious Lot

"And it's a high pop fly out to center field. Adamson fields it with no problem. Two outs in the bottom of the ninth. The Mountain Goats are down by one. The tying run is at third base, and Jim Carlin is up at the plate. He's oh-for-four today. An unlucky game for Carlin. He struck out three times and grounded out tonight. Here's an opportunity to redeem himself and win the game for the Goats."

"You know, Bob, Carlin has never cleaned his jockstrap. For good luck, you know?"

"Well, Steve, it must not be working this season. Oh-and-one's the count, and the pitch . . . whoa! It's going back! Adamson's at the warning track! It could be . . . no! Adamson makes the jump and snags the ball at the end of his glove! A miracle play that proves the powers-that-be are not Goats fans."

#

Carlin slammed his fist into his locker. "Dammit! We should've won!"

"Take it easy, Jimmy." It was the manager, Skip Slater. "We're only three games out of first, and another couple of weeks left in the season. We can still make it."

"The ball should've been out of here! That damned Anderson!"

"Shouldn't we have won today, Skipper?" asked the first baseman, Leon Mason. "Didn't we . . . ?"

Carlin groaned. "Goddammit! We forgot!"

It dawned on Skip's face. "I knew we were forgetting something. We'll have to remember for tomorrow."

"Hey Skipper!" It was Billy Hacken, the pitching coach. "The press is here!"

"I'll be right there," Skip said. "Remember for tomorrow, Carlin."

"Sure thing, Skipper."

Skip abandoned the locker room to give his usual hundred-and-ten-percent speech. There was always some joker sportswriter who wanted to comment on the players' superstitions, and that day was no exception. Skip had his work cut out for him, fielding questions about Carlin's jockstrap, Mason's lucky glove, Gruber's mismatched socks, and so on. When asked as to why they were so conscious about these silly things, Skip said, "What can I say? Us baseball players are a superstitious lot."

#

The next day, before the game, the Mountain Goats crowded the locker room. Skip held a helmet in his hands.

"All right, everybody. Line up. You know the drill." When everyone was in place, he shook the helmet slightly, reached in, and pulled out a folded sheet of paper. Once unfolded, he saw it was blank.

He went down the line of ball players, letting each one take a folded piece of paper at random. Each one was blank.

Skip was almost to the end when Jackson Maleck, the closing pitcher, unfolded his paper to find a black dot.

"Looks like we have our winner," Skip said. "You know what to do, Jackson."

"You bet, Skipper."

"You won't chicken out?"

He shook his head. "You know how much I want this pennant."

Skip clapped Maleck on the back. "Good man."

#

Not fifteen minutes later, Shirley Maleck arrived at the stadium. She was greeted by her husband in the parking lot, which was just starting to get full.

"I drove here as fast as I could," she said. "What's the emergency?"

"Follow me," Maleck said. He led Shirley to the locker room. Inside, the Mountain Goats sat around, naked except for their jockstraps. None of them seemed embarrassed by her arrival.

Shirley, on the other hand, was mortified.

"It's all right, honey," Maleck said. "I brought her, Skip."

Skip, his hairy boulder of a gut hanging over his jockstrap, stepped up behind Shirley.

"What's going on here?" she asked.

"Sorry, honey," Maleck said, "but we really need to win a few games. We're up against New York today, and we don't want to blow it."

Every team member produced a baseball. Maleck and Skip stepped aside, and everyone circled around her.

"Jackson, what is--?"

A hail of baseballs descended upon her, splitting open her lips and popping out her teeth. When there were no more balls to throw, the players took up their bats and, in batting order, took a swing at her one at a time. By the time the pitcher had his turn, she'd fallen to the floor, her body crushed in as if she had been made out of cardboard. Wet, bloody cardboard.

"All right, Jackson," Skip said, "clean up your wife. The rest of you, suit up and get on the field for practice. Game time's in a half an hour."

#

"Top of the ninth, two outs. A runner on first. Danny "Marshal" Dillon's up at the plate. Marshal takes a few practice swings and steps into the batter's box. Maleck shakes off some signals he doesn't like."

"You know, Bob, Maleck's had quite the season. Just this game, he's racked up ten strike-outs, and he's working on his fortieth save. I hear he steps onto the mound only on his left foot. For good luck, you know?"

"Well, Steve, baseball players are a superstitious lot."

"You can say that again, Bob."

"Dillon swings and misses for strike two. Boy, Mike Kelly must be sweating up a storm in New York's dugout. The Goats are only up by one. If Dillon makes this next pitch a homerun, it could just put another nail in the Goats' coffin.

"Maleck winds up, and the pitch . . . Dillon goes down swinging! The Goats win it, five to four! How about that!"

#

Maleck stepped into the locker room, surrounded by his teammates, all praising him to Hell and back again.

Skip slapped him on the back.

"Helluva game, Jackson. Great work."

"Thanks, Skipper."

# Slummin' It

He sat on the sidewalk in his own filth, a cloud of flies lingering around his greasy, unwashed, pallid body. His clothes were thick and ratty and rank. Toes with jagged nails poked out the torn ends of his loafers, and he held a Styrofoam cup with an assortment of change within. His eyes, bloodshot and slightly obfuscated with the beginnings of cataracts, were alert, shifting back and forth.

At long last, he saw what he was looking for: a man in a suit, fresh from the Stock Exchange, rushed by, his briefcase swinging with his sweeping gait like a pendulum. As he passed, the businessman's eyes glanced at the bum before intensely looking away.

The bum scampered after him, a pronounced limp in his step. "Spare some change?" he called out.

"No. Sorry." The businessman started walking faster.

The bum grasped his target's left arm at the elbow, dragging him to a stop. "C'mon, buddy. Can't ya' spare nothing?"

The businessman jerked himself from the bum's grip, then held the crook of his arm, as if he thought the derelict before him would, given a chance, steal his appendage. "Get a job, you fucking loser." This imperative was delivered in a clipped tone before the businessman strode away, not quick enough to betray his fear, not slow enough to be casual.

The bum laughed and debated pestering the businessman further. He decided against it. While the suit denoted a man with a taste for human flesh, this sorry example of a person didn't seem to have a predilection for violence. He made for an excellent appetizer, though; there would no doubt be something better down the line.

He shuffled his way through the streets until he came upon a black man dressed in the finest gangsta chic money could buy, bopping his head to whatever music the iPod had plugged into his ears.

The bum turned around so he could walk at the black man's side. "Hey, brother, spare some change?" He held out a supine hand, which was stained with shit, as he could find no newspaper with which to wipe his ass after his morning constitutional.

The black man stopped and pulled his headphones out. "Fuck you, white boy. I ain't yo' 'brother,' a'ight?" When he said "brother," he pumped the index and middle fingers of each hand to indicate quotation marks.

"C'mon, man, just a little something-something? You're wearing all this bling." Here, it was the bum's turn to illustrate his point with finger-quotation marks. "And I got shit. Please, man, I'm hungry."

"Oh, you hongry?" the black man asked as he lifted his middle finger. "Eat this." Without another comment, he continued on his way.

Better. Not the ideal response, but closer.

Time passed. The occasional person dropped change into his cup. Most ignored him. A precious few took the valuable time out of their lives to berate him, but no one presented the gift he truly desired. As the hour hand on the park clock crept toward three, he decided he had to do something drastic.

He waited until he saw the perfect candidate: a young man with muscles large enough to make Lou Ferrigno sick, decked out in a sweat-marked jogging suit, though he was now walking and holding two fingers to his throat, probably between mile runs. The jock wore a grimace like most punks did, trying to convince the world they were tough.

The bum, not exactly the healthiest of specimens, nearly had to jog to keep up with the jock. "Spare some . . . ." He had to stop to catch his breath a moment. "Spare some change, buddy?"

"Beat it," the jock said without looking at him, eyes firmly focused on the ass of a woman bent over, scooping up the pile of shit her poodle had just left on the ground. The jock licked his lips and nodded, lost in fantasy.

The bum felt it necessary to destroy his companion's daydream. He pawed at the jock's Nike shirt, grasping for purchase and finding very little. "Please! I need a fix! I'll do anything! You want a blow-job? I'll do that! Be a sport, huh?"

The jock's steroid-addled thought processes were a little slow to break away from coital visions, but when he realized what was happening, he stumbled to a halt and pushed the bum away. "Get off!" he grunted as the bum fell to the grass. It looked like his assailant was going to stay down, so he uttered a laugh and continued on his way.

The bum said one word that made him stop: "Faggot."

It worked just as well as if he'd cast a spell. The jock whirled around and rushed the bum, who was still sitting on the ground. With a deft kick, he broke the bum's nose and knocked his front teeth down his throat. There was a gagged cry of pain, but that didn't stop the jock from wrapping his fist in the bum's torn lapel and yanking him to his feet. Ignoring the blood now spattered on his forearm, the jock laid into his target twice with his free hand.

"Who's the fag now, huh?" The jock released the bum, who crumpled to the ground in a shapeless mass, more like a pile of dirty laundry than a human being.

As soon as the jock was gone, the bum sat up and started laughing. People looked at him in shock, and mothers turned their children away from the spectacle. Dogs barked nervously and cowered behind their owners. Joggers made sure to give him plenty of room as they went around him and tried not to look.

Finally! He'd gotten what he wanted! Blissful pain! How could something so wonderful be so elusive? Was this the ritual he had to perform in order to receive this greatest of gifts?

#

Sleeping in the alley was fun, covered only with the clothes on his back and the sports section from Sunday's edition of the paper. The hard, cold ground pressed against his back, causing him to wake up with a crick in his neck that just wouldn't crack. He couldn't help but smile.

He waited until about noon before he went back to the park. Today, he had a wonderful plan, a plan so well-conceived it couldn't fail. All he had to do was wait for all the required ingredients to align, and he was certain he'd be in the hospital by sundown.

When he got to the fountain, he sat on the stone ledge and paddled his hands through the water, gazing down at the pennies littering the bottom like confetti on New Year's Eve. There was a group of kids playing tag nearby, so all he needed was a cop.

His wish was granted ten minutes later. Eagerly, he pulled his pants down to his ankles, hung his ass over the ledge, and theatrically pushed with all his might. He grunted and strained and forced his face to go red. Through his slitted eyes, he noticed he had the attention of the kids. They all pointed at him just as he defecated with a pleasant splash. The girls, horrified, turned away as the boys laughed like hyenas with about as much class.

The bum singled out a pudgy, bespectacled girl. "Got any toilet paper, kid?"

The cop was at his side in record time. "Pull your goddam pants up. There's kids here, for Christ's sake."

The bum slid off the stone ledge, leaving a brown streak where his ass touched it. "Sorry, officer. When ya' gotta' go . . . ."

"Just go," the cop said. "Get the hell outta' here. Don't let me see you around here again."

As the bum pulled up his pants, he searched the cop's eyes for violence. It was clear he wanted to use his nightstick, but there was something else in there the bum hadn't counted on: concern for the children. This pathetic excuse for a cop didn't want to brutalize a man in front of kids. Upon seeing this lack of initiative, the bum couldn't help but wonder if the guy would lose his job for being a nice guy.

For the next couple of days, no one committed a violent act upon him, no matter how grotesque he became. Very few had more to offer than some choice words, even when he stopped in the middle of traffic just to take a leak. The hippie in the classic Beetle offered only an indulgent smile, nothing more. He didn't even honk the horn. Had society fallen so far that you could insult a man to his face and be answered with a shrug? Didn't anyone have pride anymore?

He didn't know it at the time, but the few days of disappointment would be worth what came later. In fact, he was ready to call it quits and go home when humanity was redeemed in his eyes by a young, fashionable sadist.

The bum was asking change of people leaving a nightclub when a blond-haired, blue-eyed golden boy exited, accompanied by a gaggle of frat boys. He looked at their leader, a well-tuned alpha male of the first order, dressed in a turtleneck and a sweater bearing Greek symbols. His sports jacket was open despite the cool evening air, and a scarf hung from his shoulders, more out of pretentiousness than actual need, as it was only fall. The hard, angular features of his face denoted a man of quiet, well-calculated violence. A winner.

The bum stepped into the golden boy's path and said, "Spare some change, pal? I'll do anything for some change."

The golden boy smiled, showing angel-white, small teeth, much like a piranha's. "Anything?"

"Damn straight. I need some junk."

"Would you eat garbage from a hospital dumpster?"

"Aw, Brad!" one of his companions said. "That's fucked up!"

"Do it everyday," the bum said.

"That's no fun, then," Brad said. "How about a turd? Would you eat a turd?"

"Done it."

Brad and his friends laughed; it sounded like a pack of beasts roaming the jungle for their prey. "Okay," their leader said. "Would you take a punch for a quarter?"

"Done it for less."

"Would you blow me? Plus a rim job?"

"Dude!" another friend exclaimed. "Don't say shit like that!"

"Absolutely," the bum said. "Let you cum on my face, too. I don't care."

Raucous groans filled the night air, mixed with self-conscious laughter and shouted epithets meant to shame the bum. Brad remained silent as he seemingly considered the proposition. Then, he said, "What do you think I am? Queer? Do I come off as gay?"

The bum shrugged. "You made the offer, buddy. Looks faggoty to me."

Brad's friends turned their laughter onto him. "Got you there, motherfucker!" one crowed. "Bam!" another shouted. "You gonna' take that shit from him?" a third inquired. Their leader only offered his piranha smile, and the bum knew the gauntlet was down.

"Okay, okay," Brad said slowly. "I got a good one. Would you cut off your own hand and eat it?"

The bum felt his loins lengthen and press against his baggy, torn pants. Here it was! The moment for which he'd been searching for days! "Sure," was all he could manage as his throat constricted with excitement.

Brad's eyebrows lifted into Satanic, inverted V's. "Are you serious?"

"I need my fix," the bum said, hopping from foot to foot. "I've got two hands, anyway. All I need's one."

The frat boys broke out into their primitive, tribal laughter, but Brad was too busy reaching into his pocket to waste time on hilarity. He pulled out a ten dollar bill. "You'd do it for this?"

The bum fell to his knees and kissed Brad's moneyed hand. "You're a saint, sir. At the left hand of God, you are."

Brad gazed down, as if he were Jesus Christ Himself, and patted the penitent bum's head as if he were forgiving him of his sins. With his other hand, he reached into his pocket and produced a Swiss Army knife. The blade was small but looked sharp enough. He pressed it into the bum's grip and said, "Let's go down the alley so no one sees us."

"Whoa! Hold on," one of his friends said, touching Brad's shoulder. "You're not really going to let him do it, are you?"

Brad shook himself free. "Hell yeah, I am. That's good entertainment for ten bucks. Would you rather rent a movie? When are we going to get a chance like this again?"

No one else objected as they retreated down the alley, where the bum sat on the ground and began rolling up his sleeve. In the dim glow from the neon signs of the nightclub, they all watched, twitching and laughing as the bum put the knife to his wrist. He looked up at the others and felt a nervous squirt of acid burn the back of his throat. Never before had he gone this far, and the feather tickling the inside of his stomach went wild with anticipation.

"Haven't got all night," Brad said, crossing his arms. His bored eyes betrayed his thoughts to the bum, who suddenly realized this sadist didn't believe he'd go through with it.

He pressed on the flat end of the blade and drew the edge across his veins. At first, there was only a little blood oozing around the knife, but when he moved it forward in a sawing fashion, gore shot from his flesh as if his arm were a hose. The frat boys jumped back to avoid being splashed, their groans and laughter a cacophony to rival even the most vociferous of dog packs. Brad remained silent and watchful.

Next to go were the tendons, and the fingers on the nearly disembodied hand went limp. The bum showed a mouthful of broken teeth as he reveled in exquisite pain. Yet it wasn't this burning sting that brought him pleasure; it was the sensation of the cold metal parting his soft, buttery flesh.

He worked around the bones until they were all that held his hand in place. Laughter ripped from his throat as he forced the blade down. There was a crack, and his hand rolled away to the pavement like a misshapen ball.

A couple of frat boys puked while the rest turned away except one, who remained at Brad's side, his mouth open in awe. "Dude! I can't believe he did it!"

Brad rubbed his chin. "I can. He had a look in his eyes."

The bum scooped up his hand and looked at it. Had this really been a part of him mere moments ago? It seemed more like a prop for a horror movie than the real thing, but there it was. Still warm. Still dripping. He held it next to his gushing stump, fascinated by the jagged knob of bone that jutted from the end.

"Look at all that blood," he muttered. "That's me dying, I think."

Brad didn't hear him. "Don't forget about the second part of our deal."

"Gimme fire, so I can cook it."

"Whoa, uh-uh." Brad's arms crossed again, and he shook his head. "That wasn't part of it. It's got to be raw."

"My teeth are infirm," the bum said, opening his mouth. "I can't eat it like this."

Brad examined the chompers in question, as if he were a Roman assessing the value of a slave. He sighed and turned to his friends. "Okay, guys, get some newspapers together. Enough to cook over. And hurry. It doesn't look like he's got much time left."

The bum tied his belt around the wound to staunch the bleeding; it slowed to a trickle, which still wasn't safe, but it was all he needed. As soon as the frat boys had gathered an adequate supply of newspapers stuffed into a garbage can, they lit it on fire with lighter fluid.

Light-headed, the bum stabbed his severed hand and twisted the blade until there was a ragged hole in the middle. Through this, he slid a stick and held it over the flames.

"Dude," said one of the frat boys. "How do you like your hand? Medium rare?"

There were a few distracted laughs as everyone watched the dead flesh turn brown. The air was suddenly redolent of greasy steak, surprisingly appetizing. More than a few mouths filled with saliva in that alley.

When he deemed it ready, the bum didn't hesitate in the slightest. He sank his teeth in the steaming meat. Hot juice ran down his chin as he chewed his first mouthful of human flesh. There were many depraved things he'd experienced in life, but this one was new to him. He enjoyed every succulent bite. When he was done, he dropped the bones into the guttering fire.

"What did it taste like?" Brad asked.

"Chicken, dude!" one of his buddies said.

Brad groaned. "That's an old one. Stupid, too."

"Tastes like rattlesnake," the bum said, just to be funny.

Everyone laughed, and Brad said, "Good show, old boy." He handed over the ten dollars. "Worth every penny. Spend it as you will."

Brad led his gaggle of frat boys away, giggling and regaling one another with the details of what they'd just witnessed. Only one didn't follow, the one who hadn't puked or turned away when the hand came off. "Why would you do something like that?" he asked. "And enjoy it? I saw you smiling."

"It's only flesh," the bum said. He licked his meat-moistened lips.

The frat boy looked down at the bum, uncertain as the others had been. "Are you going to be okay? You need a hospital?"

"I'm better off than you," the bum wheezed.

"Come on, Paul!" Brad shouted. "Leave that scumbag alone! Let's get some pussy!"

Paul cast one more look back at the bum before he left to follow the others. Only then did the bum allow himself to collapse face down. He couldn't even feel the sharp pebbles sticking into his pale cheek as the world began to fade around him.

"Okay," he muttered. "I'm ready to come home now."

The world flashed around him, as if a lightning storm had formed out of nowhere. It felt like someone was pinching the inside of his head, and his vision blinked out. When he opened his eyes, he was back in his own body, watching as the doctor removed the wires taped to his temples.

"Did you enjoy your vacation?" the doctor asked.

"I had a blast! You wouldn't believe what happened!"

"Of course I'd believe. I monitored everything, which

includes what happened just after I brought you back. The street person expired seven seconds later."

"That cost extra?"

"Naturally. It was in the contract, if you'll recall. The street person has a wife who must be reimbursed."

"How much?"

"It'll cost another million."

"It's damn well worth it." He took out his checkbook. "Who do I make this out to?"

"Out of Body Vacations, Inc."

He filled out the check, ripped it from his book, and handed it over. "Doc, you're a genius. I've never felt so alive before."

"I'm sure," the doctor said. "Thanks for using Out of Body Vacations, and we hope to hear from you again very soon."

*"You can count on it.*

# A Night in the Unlife

THUMP! THUMP! THUMP!

"Mommy! Daddy! Wake up! We hungry!"

Rich opened his eyes. Stella, his wife, already sat up in bed next to him. "What time is it, honey?" he asked.

Stella looked at the alarm clock. "Seven-fifteen."

"Damn. The sun's not even down yet."

"We might as well feed them."

"You feed them. Saturdays are the only nights I can sleep in."

"All right, all right." Stella pushed the lid of their double coffin up and pulled herself out. "Okay, children. Let's see what we can find for you."

Stella pulled on her robe and followed the energetic Billy and Suzy to the kitchen. She opened the refrigerator and groaned when she saw that the pitcher of blood had only an inch left.

"What is it, Mommy?" Suzy asked.

Stella ignored her. "Riiiiiich! We're out of blood! Would you go to the store and get some?" Then, she remembered the kids were listening. She hastily added, "Please?"

Rich rubbed his eyes and moaned. "All right, Stella. All right." Why did this kind of thing always happen on Saturdays? He would have been more than happy to do it on a weekday—-on a weekday, he'd be up and ready for work by now—-but on a Saturday?

Still, he dragged himself up out of his coffin and went to the bathroom. He rubbed at his head, feeling that his dark hair was disheveled, and he knew his eyes weren't even glowing red. He ran his hand against thick stubble on his cheeks. He held a hand to his mouth and nose and exhaled. His breath smelled like a rotting corpse.

The whiskers he could live with, but his fangs needed a good brushing, and he was damned if he would go out without a shower. Besides, he had to give the sun time to finish its descent.

When he finished in the bathroom, it was dark outside. After he got dressed, he gave Stella a peck on the cheek and stepped out the front door.

The neighborhood Rich and his family lived in was pretty decent. There was a long line of sprawling, dark castles on each side of the road; each was pleasantly covered in cobwebs and made up of twisting and crooked angles, topped by pinnacles where bats lived. The property values were very high.

However, elevated above the castles, perched on a nearby mountain, sat a square house with a roof made of one angle. There wasn't so much as a cobweb on it, and the outside had wind chimes and lawn gnomes and other yard decorations. Rich had heard stories about that place —ghastly stories—but he didn't like to dwell on them.

He heard a retched, tired cranking sound and turned to his right. His neighbor yanked on a lawnmower cord, swearing under his breath.

"Hi Sam," Rich said.

Sam released the cord and smiled, showing his fangs.

"Hi-ya Rich. How's unlife treating you?"

"Ah, the wife told me she's out of blood. So she wakes me up out of a decent slumber and tells me to go get it now. The kids are hungry."

"I won't hold you up, then. This damn mower's giving me trouble, so I'll catch you later."

"If it's still not working when I get back, I'll take a look at it. I used to repair lawnmowers when I was a kid. For the old man."

"I'd appreciate it, Rich. Thanks."

They said their goodbyes, and Rich got into his car.

The grocery store sold a vast variety of blood. Different types from different creatures. Personally, Rich didn't like thinking about where his blood came from. He knew the unpleasant things that happened in slaughterhouses, but still, like the house on the mountain, he didn't like to dwell on it.

He grabbed a few bottles and, as an afterthought, added a couple of low-fat gallons to his shopping cart. When he made it to the check-out line, the clerk (who also owned the store) eyed the low-fat blood.

"What the hell's this for?" Gil asked.

Rich sighed. "The wife. She wants me to watch my waist-line." He patted his belly, which was considerably bigger than it had been in his lawnmower-repairing days.

Gil grunted and shook his head while he rang it up. "I'm proud of my paunch. It's a fuel tank for a sex machine." He laughed. "Like it says on the shirt."

Rich didn't know anything about the shirt, so he said nothing as he paid up and headed for home. Once the blood had been delivered, Rich headed over to Sam's lawn, where his neighbor still battled with the rusty old beast.

As Rich examined the mower, Sam brought out a couple of cans of blood (on the sides, they said in big letters, "BAC: 20%!!!"). Rich thanked him and drank deeply.

Sam backhanded a red mustache away. "You figure it out yet?"

"I think there's something clogged in the fuel line," Rich said. "It could take a while."

"Thanks again, Rich. I don't want to think about how much it'd cost to bring 'er into the shop."

As Rich worked, they talked and drank their way through a total of ten bloods. Sam got a bit tipsy, and as was his habit in such a condition, he ranted about the president, who was a "damn Republican who couldn't find his pooper with both hands, a flashlight, double-joints, and a scout to guide him."

Somewhere along the way, Billy and Suzy came out to the front yard to play. Billy wanted to play catch, and Suzy wanted to have a tea party, so they argued quite a bit. Rich had to interrupt his work countless times to try to get them to compromise. "And don't call your sister names, Billy. Say you're sorry."

Rich was almost done working the blockage out when he heard Stella calling for the kids. Was it lunchtime already? He cursed under his breath, wiping a sheen of bloodsweat from his forehead. Perhaps he was getting too old for this kind of thing, and Stella constantly calling Billy's name wasn't helping Rich very much.

"Billy!" he shouted. "Listen to your mother when he calls you!" He'd never raised a hand to his child, but he certainly felt like doing so now.

"Rich, have you seen Billy?" Stella asked.

"Sure, he's with Suzy."

"Suzy says Billy's gone."

"What?" Rich stood and wiped his forehead again, looking around for his son. Suzy stood by her mother, but Billy was nowhere to be seen. "Suzy, where'd Billy go?"

"He got mad at me," Suzy said. She petted her doll's head. "He hates playing tea time, so he left."

Rich knelt down so he could look Suzy in the eye. "Where did you see him go?"

Suzy absently pointed down the street. When Rich turned to follow the path of her finger, he felt his stomach drop.

Billy had gone to the square house on the mountain.

"Are you sure?" Rich asked.

"What's the problem, Rich?" Sam asked.

"Positive," Suzy said.

Rich turned back to his wife. Stella's eyes had paled to pink, and her lips hung open in a frightened grimace. "Weren't you watching the kids?" she asked, her voice shaking.

He was struck indignant for a moment, but looking at Stella's fearful face quelled the feeling. "I'm sorry, honey." He cleared his throat. "I'm going after him."

Sam approached the family, a can of blood still in his hand. "Did I hear right? Billy's missing?"

"Yeah." Rich rubbed his dirty hands on his pants. "Suzy said she went up to . . . the house on the hill."

"Up there?" Sam pointed with his drink to the square house.

"I'm going up after him," Rich said.

"Hold up. It's too dangerous to go up there alone. Haven't you heard the stories?"

Of course Rich had heard the stories. A lone human being lived up there, fueled only by the urge to kill vampires curious enough to wander up to its house. Their ghosts, it was said, walked the mountain, searching for a path back home. Sometimes, during the day, it came down to the village, armed with a stake and garlic, so it could claim more victims. Citizens died in town, and no one could explain it. Although the police had been urged on more than one occasion to do something about the human, they were too afraid to make a move.

"I have to go," Rich said. "Billy's my son."

"Then let me help," Sam said. "I know some people from my time in the war. These guys are afraid of nothing."

"We don't have the time. I have to go now."

"Okay, fine," Sam said. "You start out now, and I'll go to town. They all drink at the same place, and they're always around. We'll catch up to you, okay?"

Rich didn't want to argue, and he knew help would come in handy. "All right, fine. But hurry up. I'm going now."

#

The path up the mountain wasn't a very pleasant one, filled with bumps and rocks, as it was not paved. For the first time since he'd bought it, Rich was glad for the Hummer most vampires gave him dirty looks for owning.

The going may have been made easier by his choice in vehicle, but the sights were downright ugly. Trees that grew in full bloom, not a leaf missing from thick, healthy trunks. A sparkling stream filled with large, unappetizing fish, which the human no doubt fed upon. Living animals, from which the town's blood supply probably came. How could Billy get this far? *Did* Billy get this far?

Rich parked the Hummer in front of the gate that marked the boundary of the human's land. It was a hideous, white-washed picket . . . thing! He felt his flesh crawl as the sight of such a hideous artifice.

Taking a deep breath, he left the keys in the ignition (just in case) and got out of the car, ready to approach the fence. There was the sudden urge to turn around and forget about Billy, but Rich, horrified that such a cowardly streak ran down his spine, forced himself forward until his hand rested on the gate's latch. He pushed it open.

The legends were true. Sickening displays were rooted in the perfect lawn that preceded the square house. Pink flamingos, gnomes, jockeys, and a ceramic gathering of happy bunnies waited to greet him. Jingling at the windows was a series of wind chimes made from glass and metal tubes. A flag bearing a sun with a smiley face waved from the peak of the roof.

Keeping a careful watch over everything, he eased his way up the walk that led to the front door. Rich expected the lawn decorations to leap to life, hungry for his blood, but they remained stationary.

*Moment of truth.* He stopped on the porch. Slowly, he pulled the screen door back and placed his hand on the brass doorknob. It would not turn.

There had to be another way in. He looked to his right and left, looking for windows that could open. When he saw none, he stepped down to the lawn to head around back.

That was when the door jerked open, and the human made its appearance. In one hand, it held a string of garlic, in the other, a cross. Its flesh was full of vibrant color, and its teeth were flat, probably to inflict more pain on its victims.

"Where's my son?" Rich said. His sharp fingernails dug into his palms.

"Go back to your town, vampire," the human said. "Or I will set your ashes to the wind." It did not move from behind the threshold.

And that was when Rich realized, to his surprise, that the human was afraid of *him!* "Come out from the protection of your house, human. It's going to be hard to kill me from there."

"I have all the time in the world," the human said. "You have until sunrise. I think I have all the power here."

"Dad!" The cry came from behind the human, from within the square house.

"Billy!" Rich shouted. "Are you all right?"

"Garlic!" Billy cried. "I'm surrounded by garlic!"

Rich rushed back up the porch until he pressed against the invisible barrier that kept him from entering the human's house. "Let him go!"

The human didn't even flinch. Its lips pulled back into an evil smile, and it placed the cross onto Rich's cheek.

It burned only for a second. Rich recoiled, holding the blister that now rose from his cold flesh. He was too shaken to do anything else.

"Would you care to try again, vampire?" the human asked. The cross and garlic were now replaced by a stake and mallet.

Rich felt red tears running down his face. He'd failed his son. He'd failed his family. How could he have been so stupid? Did he seriously believe he could march up the mountain like a knight out of the King Arthur stories, slay the monster, and save the child? He hadn't even brought a weapon.

"Go back to town," the human said again. "You can save yourself for one night. But I know where you live, and I will visit you in the day."

Rich almost felt like doing just that, but then his ears detected something the human's couldn't possibly hear: the sound of a Jeep ascending the mountain. Sam and his army buddies. There was hope yet!

It wasn't long before the human got the idea. "What's that?" he asked.

The Jeep came to an abrupt stop, and about five very large, very muscular vampires leapt to the ground, each bearing either a torch or a pitchfork except for Sam, who held a crossbow.

"I command you away from here!" the human shrieked. It didn't matter. He may have been able to protect himself, but his power did not extend beyond the threshold.

Rich, stronger now with the presence of allies, marched up the porch steps until he was barely out of the human's reach. "Send out my son, and perhaps we'll let you live."

"You can't kill me," the human said. "Without me to take away the garlic from your son, he'll be stuck in there forever.

"That may be true," Sam said, "but all we want is the boy. If you hand over the kid, we'll go away. If you're not going to give him to us, we'll burn you out and kill you." He leveled the crossbow at the human's heart.

"You'll kill the boy," the human said. "Vampires hate fire just as much as me."

"Look, no one has to die," Rich said. "Just let me have Billy, and everyone will live happily ever after." He threw a glance at Sam, to make sure he wasn't going to say anything more.

The human faltered for the first time, now looking at the torches. The stake and mallet lowered slowly until they hung limply at its sides. "I have your word you'll go away?" it asked Rich.

"I swear, the instant you give me my son, I'll leave you unharmed," Rich said.

"Rich!" Sam said. "What are you saying? Don't you know how dangerous this . . . this *thing* is?"

"Sam, it's the only way." Rich turned back to the human. "I swear it."

The human nodded, then vanished from the door. The next moment, Billy bounced over the threshold and into his father's arms.

"Billy!" Rich cried. He hugged his son to his chest as hard as he could.

"Dad! It was horrible! He was gonna' kill me before you showed up! He invited me in! He told me he was gonna' give me blood candy!"

Rich considered going back on his word for a moment, but he decided not to. He'd won, after all. Billy was safe, and they were going home. "I never want you to come here again," he said to his son. "Why did you do it in the first place?"

"Suzy dared me to," Billy said. "After I called her names."

Rich thought he would have to have a little chat with

Suzy when he got back. He nodded to his friend. "Thanks, Sam. I couldn't have done this without you guys."

Sam nodded. "I'll see you back home. The boys and I are going to get some blood in town, okay? You're welcome to join us."

"Maybe another time. I owe you all at least a few drinks."

"You know it."

Rich carried Billy to the Hummer, and they started down the path to home.

Sam looked at his friends. "Well, we're here anyway. You know this creature's going to be more trouble down the line. Who knows how many good vampires it has killed already?"

The retired soldiers holding the torches knew what Sam meant. They advanced on the house and threw the flames onto the roof and through the windows.

Sam trained the crossbow on the front door and waited.

# Yum

She looked like such a small, fragile young woman. How could we have known?

You sure you want to know what happened? Because it's kind of gruesome and . . . well, crazy. I guess you're used to both, though, aren't you?

Okay, it went down like this:

My father died over the weekend. Heart attack. No need to be sorry. I didn't know him all that well. I have a few memories of him from when I was a kid, but he set out for New York to make a name for himself in banking when I was ten, and I haven't seen him since. Alive, anyway. Mom kept a sporadic contact with him, which is why I guess his new wife called to tell Mom he was dead. The new wife fought tooth and claw, but in the will Dad left, he clearly stated that he wanted to come home to be buried.

Her name? Oh, something cutsey. I don't remember. I'm sure Mom can tell you.

Anyway, Dad's body was on display at the funeral home. Just about everyone was there. Mom, Carl and Dave—they're my brothers—a bunch of aunts and uncles, and a young woman I had never seen before. My mother told me it was Dad's new wife. She was so small and bony she looked anorexic. I could probably fit my hand around her entire waist, she was that skinny. She also looked pretty young. Much younger than Dad.

Mom told me I should introduce myself to her. Of course, I wanted nothing to do with this stranger, but before I could even object, Mom put her "obey me" face on. You know the type. I sighed and said I would. "Be nice," she added.

I offered the new wife my condolences, but she didn't even acknowledge me. I didn't think it was strange; just because I didn't love my father didn't mean no one else did. Besides, this was his new wife. Dad wasn't all that rich, so she couldn't have married him for his money.

I left her alone, and we all sat down to hear my uncle give a eulogy. It was okay, I guess. Maybe if Dad had stuck around when I was a kid, I'd have felt it more.

After that, we all lined up to pay my father last respects. I got behind Dad's new wife, and my brothers and Mom got behind me. The wait wasn't long, considering how few people Dad knew. Before long, his new wife shuffled up to the open casket, and I waited for my turn, trying to think of something to say, or think, or pray.

As she leaned over to kiss Dad's cheek, I went through the possibilities. I could be mean or nice. I could call his corpse a bastard, and for once, I'd have the last word. Or I could send him off with an all's well, you know? Or maybe I could pray for his soul. I don't know.

Ahead of me, Dad's new wife was crying so hard her body shook with the force. After about a minute of this, Mom reached around my brothers and nudged me. "See if she's okay."

Of course, I didn't want to, but she read it on my face instantly. The "obey me" look reappeared, and before she could tell me to be nice again, I nodded and stepped toward the casket.

I was about to touch the new wife's shoulder and ask how she was doing, but before I could so much as lift a hand, I saw what she was doing.

How could it have been real? God, I've never seen something so . . . hideous.

Dad's new wife was eating his face. Already his nose was a gaping hole, and his lips had been torn away, revealing Dad's teeth back to his molars. A swath of his cheek had given away to shining bone, and good God, she was trying to suck his eyeballs out.

God, I'm crying. Never thought I'd shed a single tear for Dad.

I stood there, unbelieving. I wondered if I was just having some kind of nightmare. There was no way this could be real, or so I thought.

The scream was out of my mouth before I realized it. Everyone jumped around me, and the mood was no longer somber. I could almost hear the people saying, "Oh, look at poor Mark. He's not handling it well. He's going crazy. But who could blame him?"

Mom looked absolutely mortified, not because of Dad's new wife——she couldn't see Dad's face yet——but because of me. I could tell because horror quickly turned to anger, as if I was just a kid and I'd misbehaved.

By then, Dad's new wife had pulled herself away from the casket. Flaps of Dad's skin——I could barely believe that's what they were——hung from her mouth, and her lips were stained with some kind of liquid. I guess it was embalming fluid. I don't know.

Only then did everyone else see why I was screaming, and they joined me. The funeral director was frozen. I'm sure he's never seen anything like that before, in all of his career. There are all kinds of ways to grieve, but cannibalism can't be too frequent a method.

Mom started raving, but I couldn't understand what she was saying, except for the curse words.

Uncle Josh rushed to the new wife. A million questions

jumped from his mouth, but the new wife didn't answer. She just pushed him away.

Then, I stepped forward, but when she growled, I backed away. She bent over the casket and started eating Dad again.

Uncle Josh, assisted by Uncle Charlie and Uncle Ben, managed to wrestle the new wife away from Dad, but she was fighting hard. That was about the time you guys showed up and arrested her.

Do any of you know why she did that . . . stuff? No? It doesn't make sense to me, either. I guess that there's a lot of craziness in the world.

#

An excerpt from the report of Detective Lieutenant Cameron Laurich:

Strangest of all is what happened to Lucy Jones after her detainment. She had been in our custody for several hours before Officer Hart went to check on her. He discovered her corpse. She'd managed to tear her straight jacket off. Both legs were missing from her knees down, and her arms were gone up to the shoulders. It is my preliminary opinion that she ate herself to death.

# The Skyscraper of Suspicious Delight

1

"Just admit it, George. We're lost. We need to ask for directions."

George Penderghast gritted his teeth and tried not to look at his wife. He wasn't a violent man, and the very idea of hitting a woman was sheer insanity to him; nevertheless, he felt the urge, itching at the back of his neck like a sunburn, to bring his delicate accountant's hand across Ellen's cheek. The crisp smack alone would be worth it, but he knew the true prize would be the shocked silence that followed. That was all he wanted right now: utter silence.

"I have to go potty."

George glanced up into the rearview to see his younger son, Denny, squirming in his seat, his Game Boy DS temporarily forgotten in the grip of his tremulous hands.

Why hadn't he listened to his friends seventeen years ago? They'd warned him that marriage sucked the life out of you. You couldn't go out anymore, you couldn't hang with your friends whenever you wanted to. Things had been so much easier, so much more fun, before "I do."

*If only I could get rid of them,* he thought. *I'd have to kill them all, so I wouldn't have to pay child support, and it would have to look like an accident, but I'd be free again! I'm only forty. I can still have fun—*

Good Lord, had he actually been thinking about that? A shudder twisted through his heart. Sure, marriage sucked most of the time, but he loved his wife and kids. He had no idea what he'd do without them. The very idea of killing them churned in his stomach until he felt the back of his throat ignite with bile.

He reached to the armrest, to a roll of antacids. Steering with one hand, he picked at the wrapper with his thumbnail on the other until he freed a tablet from its prison. He flipped it into his mouth.

"Oh, look," Ellen said, pointing. "There's a gas station. Denny can use the bathroom while we ask for directions."

George looked at the gas station, a generic place that might have once been an Amoco. Behind the counter was a black man, and there were several black customers in there.

He knew it wasn't very P.C. of him, but black people made him feel uncomfortable. Growing up in the suburbs, he'd never gotten much exposure to them, and his father, who'd lived in the city when he was young, always talked about how the darker a person's skin was, the less you could trust him. George always thought that was silly, but he still couldn't help feeling nervous around black people. He wasn't about to don a white sheet and start burning crosses on lawns—in fact, he hated racists—but this was something that had been hardwired into his brain from childhood.

"I don't think so, Ellen," he said, looking back at the street. "Besides, the guy at the hotel said we could get on the expressway down here."

"Daaaaad." Denny squirmed, holding his crotch. "I

have to goooo."

"Please, George? We—"

"Besides," George continued, "have you seen the neighborhood we're in? Look around us." He waved his hands to the crumbling buildings. To the broken streetlights. To the hole-in-the-wall bars and pawn shops. To the shattered bottles and the plump woman with a skirt short enough to reveal her g-string. To the porch filled with sitting, laughing young black men. "Do you really want me to stop around here?"

"Well, I—"

"We have eight-hundred-and-ninety dollars for the rest of our vacation. Do you want us to get mugged? Miss out on Washington, DC? Go back to Indiana bruised, if we're *lucky*?"

"No, George! I—"

"You're going to have to hold it, Denny." George looked into the back seat via the rearview mirror. "Play a game with him, Jordan."

His older son didn't hear him. He was too busy listening to his iPod.

"Jordan? Take off those earphones and play a game with your little brother."

Jordan grimaced in a way only teenaged boys could achieve as he pulled the plugs out of his ears. "But, Dad!"

"Do as your father says," Ellen whispered.

"Come on, Mom! It's not my fault that—"

"Play a game with Denny. Take his mind off going pee-pee. If you do this for me, I'll let you go to Ozzfest with your friends this summer."

Jordan paused. "Really?"

"Yes."

With a sidelong glance to the back of his father's head: "Could I get that in writing?"

"Just do it, Jordan," George said. He gripped the steering wheel harder. He could feel his back starting to hunch, no matter how hard he tried to stop it.

"Let's just turn around, George," Ellen said, placing her hand on his shoulder. "It's getting dark. What's one more day in this city?"

*It'll put us behind schedule,* he was about to say, but to the right, he saw towering orange streetlights. "Look, Ellen," he said, pointing. "That's got to be the expressway over there."

Ellen looked like she wanted to argue, but the evidence of the lights was too convincing.

"Don't worry, Denny," George said into the mirror. "The first rest stop we find, we'll stop."

He turned the car at the next corner and started heading for the orange lights. He knew it was only a matter of time at this point before he found the expressway, as long as he kept the lights in view.

George saw warehouses and instantly realized he was in the wrong place. Ahead, he could see a yellow DEAD END sign and cursed under his breath.

Denny laughed. "Daddy said a bad word!"

George bit back the urge to snarl at his own child. Instead, he pulled over to the curb, ready to turn around.

"George, what are you doing?" Ellen sounded ready to panic.

"Relax, Ellen. This isn't a through-street. Didn't you see the sign?"

George completed the turn and was about to speed up when something thumped into the side of their car. Ellen uttered a startled yip, and the kids went very quiet.

"It's okay," George said. "I probably hit—"

*--the curb,* he was about to say, but he was interrupted by the sound of a shattering bottle colliding with the side of their car. Ellen screamed, and Denny started crying.

Thrown rocks pattered against the car, and one of the windows cracked. He couldn't contain himself any longer. The rage at being lost and stuck in the car with his mouthy family, and now what would probably be hundreds of dollars in damage to his car, it all boiled out of him as he savagely pounded the brake. The rotors screamed, and the car nearly fishtailed into a fire hydrant.

"No!" Ellen cried. "Keep going!"

"Goddammit!" George roared. "I've had enough of this shit!"

"It's not worth it, George! It's not worth dying over!"

George didn't hear her; he was already out the door and striding in the direction from which the projectiles had come. Distantly, he wished he'd taken his gun with him on vacation, but he figured this would be no problem. It would be a bunch of black kids, thinking they were tough. He'd yell and threaten to call the police, and maybe he'd even grab one to hold onto while Jordan called 911 from his cell phone. Either way, the black kids would be too scared to deal with a white man face to face.

Then, he saw his assailants, and his mind tripped inside his skull. He had to force his feet from walking, and he was surprised to find his throat constricted. He sucked air in through his nose to breathe.

Standing in front of him were five kids, no more than ten years old, and all of them were white. Two were even girls. All of them were well-dressed, in suits and ties, as if they were on their way to a business meeting, or a confirmation.

*Or a funeral,* George thought when he saw their weapons. The biggest kid held a baseball bat. The others held knives, rocks, and beer bottles. They were very quiet, and they were all smiling.

No, that wasn't right. All their perfect, white teeth were showing, but not in smiles. They were sneering. Battle-ready.

He felt a moment of doubt, but it passed quickly. These were only kids, no matter how they looked or what they were armed with. He could take them if worse came to worst, and right now, all he wanted to do was put the fear of God into them.

Ellen rolled down the window. "Get back in the car, George!"

He ignored her. "Listen, you little turds, I--!"

A seven-year-old girl hurled a rock into Ellen's face, striking her on the cheek. She cried out, holding her wound with one hand and frantically rolling up the window with her other.

George didn't even see Ellen. He'd heard her cry, and that was enough. He leapt forward, intent on grabbing the girl, curses rolling off his tongue like saliva, but the boy with the bat was expecting this; the Louisville Slugger met George's head with a crisp crack—-the sound of a line drive—and he went down.

He was out for only a second, and when he came back, it was to the screams of his family. He tried to stand, but he was too dazed. All he could do was watch, from a Twilight Zone slant, as his wife was dragged from the car, screaming and offering money if only the little thugs would leave them alone.

Blood crept into his vision, and he tried to blink it away, but red smeared and tinted the world. He tried to speak but could only pry a groan from his throat.

"He's still awake," one of the kids said. Enunciated perfectly.

The smallest of the bunch, maybe five years old, ran forward and with a foot encased in a dress shoe, tassels and all, kicked George in the face. The last thing he was aware of was the click of his teeth coming together, and then he was gone.

2

George came to briefly about thirty minutes later. It felt like someone was carrying him, and when he opened his eyes, he saw he'd been slung over the shoulder of the biggest kid.

*How can he lift me?* he wondered. *I'm two-hundred-and-twenty pounds!*

Still, he could feel enormous muscles coiling and uncoiling inside the kid. Looking to his left, he could see another boy dragging his wife, her arms clasped around his neck. She looked like a cloak.

Jordan walked next to them, holding Denny's hand. They were guarded by the others.

Everyone stopped, and George could hear a harsh scraping sound, almost like fingernails on a chalkboard. The bat boy then heaved and dropped George. He expected to hit the cement, and he steeled himself for it, but he felt his stomach flip when he fell down a manhole instead. This confused him so much he wasn't prepared for the rotten fart stench or the water, so when he struck the bottom, he folded into himself and left the world once again.

### 3

This time, when he came back, he found himself in a darkened, cold room, lit only by a hanging, caged light bulb eight feet above. He could feel grime on his skin and grit in his hair, but worse than the unpleasant film of filth on his body were the handcuffs on his wrists; they kept him bound to a sweaty, warm pipe.

Something moved on his chest, and he screamed for the first time in his adult life. He tried to yank his hands free to beat at the thing, but his sudden terror and squirming were enough to send it squealing away. Only then did he get a good look at it, and it made him retch when he saw it was a rat the size of a small dog.

And there were more of them nearby. They were feeding on something large. It took him a moment to see the empty eye and nose sockets. To see the gleaming face of a skull. To see they were running around in an empty rib cage. Gnawing at human bones.

And he screamed again.

He was answered by laughter. Whoever made this sound was not amused. It was too jagged a noise to be anything but hysterical.

George's eyes darted around to locate the lunatic only to find he didn't have to search far. Chained to another pipe, about ten feet away, were the ragged remains of a living man. His mouth was a laughing, dark O in the center of a nappy beard. Eyes wide enough to be half-dollars shone from the hollow pits above his sharp cheekbones. Long hair stuck to his sweaty, solitary arm, which was the only limb he had. Since he was naked, George could count the man's ribs. He could see the hollow of his belly. He could see the ragged holes where his other limbs had been.

George didn't think his companion would be able to respond, but still he tried. "Mister? Where are we?"

"Mister?!" the man shrieked. "Oh, that's so, so funny!" He laughed hard enough to make the pipes vibrate.

"Did you see where they took my family?"

The hilarity died without so much as a fade out. The stranger's crotch, ragged and bereft of genitals, pulsed. "The Master has them," he whispered.

"Who's the Master?"

"Sovereign of the Skyscraper. He likes to eat me. He says I'm his favorite!" He lowered his voice and winked at George. "I'm getting too skinny, though." A moment of quiet, and then the stranger howled, "I hope he chokes on my bones!" Tears cut down the dirt on his cheeks and his ruin of a body shook.

George looked at the ragged holes. No, no one had cut those limbs off. The cannibalism had to be this poor wretch's nightmare. In fact, this whole situation was too insane to be true. There had to be a reality TV camera crew nearby, and upon discovering them, he'd sue their asses.

And then, the stranger's crotch moved again, this time more obviously. Something dark poked out of the hole: a rat's greasy head. It was eating the stranger's insides.

"Hee-hee," the stranger wheezed. "Tickles."

George turned away and gagged into his arm. Of course someone had cut the man's arm and legs off; it was the rats that had made his wounds so ragged.

*Please God, don't let me puke,* he thought as he pressed his mouth into his bicep. *Don't let me puke. I don't know how long I'll be down here. I'll need whatever food I have in me to stay in me.*

Footsteps. The sound of good shoes clopping on the hard cement floor. George looked up to see two young men—twenty-five? thirty?—-standing over the stranger. Both wore suits under their butcher aprons, and one held a very large carving knife.

"Where's my family?" George had meant to sound tough and scary, like Clint Eastwood at his peak, but he was ashamed by the weak squeal of his pathetic voice.

One of the butcher boys turned to him. "What is the caliber of your wife's culinary talents?" The words were so well enunciated that George couldn't believe it had been done without an affected British accent.

"What?"

"Your wife. The Master wants to know if she's a good cook."

George stuttered for a moment, and he finally managed to say, "She's a great cook." Somehow, they didn't feel like words that should be spoken in this situation.

"Thank you, sir." He turned to his partner. "Let's get this over with."

They unchained the stranger, who was queerly silent, even when they sawed at his remaining appendage. They sliced the flesh around the bone and de-gloved him from shoulder to fingertips. No sound. If the stranger had felt it, he said nothing.

They then stepped on the bone until it snapped with an unsettling sound, much like someone jumping on a full bag of potato chips. The stranger grimaced at this, but still did not so much as whimper.

One butcher patted the stranger's cheeks. "Not much

here," he said. "We left him down here too long."

They turned him over and slapped his quivering, shit-smeared ass. "There's still plenty here, though."

This time, when they cut into his rump, the man screamed. George cringed and wanted to beg them to stop, but he couldn't find his voice. Even if he could, he held on to the hope that this was maybe still some sick, twisted reality show, and the stranger was just a special effect of some kind.

All he could do was look away.

"We didn't get a lot of meat from him this time," Butcher One said. "We should get his intestines, don't you think?"

"Sure," Butcher Two said. "They would probably make fine sausages."

The stranger screamed again. Then, one of the butchers said, "Could you please hold him open for me? Thank you." Something wet slapped the floor, but the sound was drowned out by the stranger's pain, and George dared not look.

Finally, the screams turned to sobs. The stranger cried silently.

"Very nice," Butcher One said. "This will make an excellent meal."

Butcher Two: "Should we put him out of his misery?"

Butcher One: "No. Why bother?"

"Hm. Do you think the people on the thirty-ninth floor will want him later?"

"Probably. We'll ask."

Footsteps again, moving away. George finally looked to see the stump that remained of his companion, shaking with tears, unable to defend himself against the rats. They already crept toward him, and before long, they gnawed at his body, and the screams began anew.

Finally, George puked. It came rushing out of him in gouts, slicking the stone floor around his head.

## 4

The man died two hours later, and only then did George shed tears of his own.

When the rats finished with the stranger, they started lapping away at George's used dinner.

## 5

George had a lot of time to think, mostly about his family. He was horrified that he'd wished them ill earlier, just before the monstrous children had attacked them. Now, all he felt was fear for their well-being. Were they even still alive?

His captors didn't feed him, so he had to lick the pipes for water, and he lasted two days before he finally gave in to the urge to eat vermin. He started small with the roaches, and then he started playing dead until the rats got close enough.

Rat wasn't so bad, once you got past the fur. Still, it was something George didn't want to remember. So, he didn't.

Every once in a while, someone checked on him. Considering what had happened to his companion, George thought it would be prudent to not rave and draw attention to himself. In fact, he thought it would behoove him to pretend weakness.

It was this kind of forward thinking, gleaned from years of reading espionage novels, that saved him when the butcher boys came for his left arm.

## 6

He heard their approach before he saw them. George had no idea how big the room was, but the echoes of their footsteps reverberated loud enough to make the pipes hum and throb. It took him a moment to shake the tension out of his body, but he finally forced himself to go slack. He curled into a fetal position with his back toward the butcher boys. The urge to peek over his shoulder was maddening, and he pushed his face into his forearms to stop himself. His belly quivered, and it took all of his effort to remain still.

"Georgie." The deep baritone voice nearly made him jump, but fear kept its choke-hold on him. If he jumped, they'd know.

"The Master has requested your presence."

"Or, part of your presence, anyway." Butcher Two laughed, but his partner remained stoic.

"I hope you're not lying about your wife's ability to cook," he said. "It would be a waste of an arm."

"No," George wheezed. "Don't." He didn't quite trust the look on his face to turn around now.

The butcher boys settled it for him. One rolled him on his back while the other reached for the handcuffs.

George's body started to tense for battle. *Not yet!* he thought. *Wait!*

He shook the tension away. Fear and pressure made him want to gnaw his own mouth off, but George didn't move until he heard the click of his cuffs being removed.

The butcher boys were big and strong, but they were bending over him—off-balance—and George had the element of surprise on his side. He lurched off the ground and grabbed a handful of Butcher One's hair. Using his own weight, he brought the giant down hard, aiming his head at the pipe. There was a short, dull gong, and Butcher One went slack.

Butcher Two, clearly the dumber of the pair, was speechless. At the last second, he tried to get his carving knife up, but it was too late. George whipped his left arm at him, the one with the handcuffs still attached. The metal claw caught Butcher Two on the cheek, opening it slightly and allowing a tiny stripe of blood to slip out.

Butcher Two screamed, harder and louder than the wound deserved, but George wasn't one to complain. Keeping one hand up to guard against the knife (in case Butcher Two came back to his senses), he lashed out with his other arm, putting a solid hook into his assailant's jaw. Butcher Two went down like a scarecrow, limbs flopping, and the knife hit the floor with a clack. George wasted no time in scooping it up and planting it in Butcher Two's throat.

George didn't think about it until Butcher Two was dead. *I just killed someone.* The body, which now seemed more like a Hollywood prop than a human being, no longer had enough life in it to make it seem real. Though he was an agnostic, he couldn't help but quail at the idea of breaking God's most important Commandment. A more sensible part of his brain tried to convince him that it had been the right thing to do, that these people had meant to cut his limbs off and eventually kill him. That he would have to do it again, to Butcher One, who was undoubtedly playing dead.

*No,* he thought. *No more killing.* He'd taken self-defense courses at the Y, but he never thought battle would be anything like this. He didn't expect the guilt.

*Stomp his head in. You won't be safe unless you kill the bastard.*

George's stomach convulsed, and he had to swallow the burn back down into his gut. He really wanted to kill the other guy, and no one would blame him if he did. Here was his chance to kill someone with no repercussions.

*What kind of fucking monster am I?* he wondered. *Stop thinking about it. Just leave. Escape.*

He tried to pull the knife out of Butcher Two's throat. It gave a little, but not much.

*You're just pulling a knife out of a log,* he thought as he looked up at the ceiling and stepped on Butcher Two's (trunk) chest and yanked the blade free. He didn't bother to wipe the blood off.

7

Much to George's surprise, there was no guard on the

cellar door. In fact, there didn't seem to be many people at all. He ran into nobody as he made his way up the stairs to the ground level. Turning the corner, he discovered a wide, tall lobby. Shiny marble floor. Freshly washed windows. Exotic plants and art. Very few people.

One person: a guard at the security desk. Could it be that he was the only person who stood between George and freedom? It seemed too easy. Cars zipped by outside. The sun was out. It looked like a nice day.

"Excuse me, sir?"

George looked up to see the security guard, an elderly gent with a wart on his nose and the worst set of oversized dentures George had ever seen; they made him look like a cartoon character. He was looking at George with his wispy eyebrows arched.

"I don't think I've seen you around here before," the guard said. "Your pass, please?"

*How does he not see my knife?* George wondered. Then, he saw the guard's holster. Hair was growing out of the pallid material. His bowels twisted, and he knew his only hope for survival was to fake the guy out.

"Oh! That!" George reached into his pocket, making like he was looking for his errant pass.

The guard relaxed a bit. In his swiftness to get to his pocket, a drop of blood sailed off the tip of the knife and spattered on the guard's shirt.

"Hey, watch it, buddy! Remember, I'm the public face of this company! Think about what would happen if one of the uninitiated accidentally wandered in here, asking for directions! What am I gonna' say, huh? Tell me that!"

"Sorry," George said. "Ah! Here it is!"

He pulled his empty hand from his pocket as the guard chided him, advising that he should wear the badge while in the building. His speech cut short when he saw George's hand was bare.

George gave him just enough time to register this before he brought the hilt of the knife down on top of the old man's bald head. The guard went down in a pile of limbs as if George had simply turned off his power switch.

*Free,* he thought. All he had to do was walk out the door, and the rats, the sadistic lunatics, the whole mess would be behind him.

*But so would my family.*

This thought was all it took; he would not leave without Ellen, Jordan, and Denny.

He knelt at the guard's side and took the gun from its human flesh holster. Once armed, he ran to the security station and reached for the phone. He decided the best thing to do would be to call the cops and then try to find his family, in case he failed and got caught. He was about to dial 911 when he heard the dial tone.

It was a baby song. "La-la-LA! La-la-LA! La-la-lalalala-la-la-LA!"

*What the fuck kind of joke is this?* he wondered. He hit 911 anyway, and when he pressed each button, a joy buzzer ERRR! sound spat from the receiver. The song then resumed.

George dropped the phone and looked at the monitors, expecting to see security footage; instead, he saw they were all on a loop. A man putting a gun in his mouth and blowing his brains out over and over. Repeated images of nuclear weapons exploding. A man getting kicked in the nuts again and again. Crusty tissues littered the floor under the desk, and George felt the desire to finish the old bastard off.

*No,* he thought. *I have to save my family, and I have to do it alone.*

He looked at the desk, hoping to find something that could help him out. With a smile, he opened a book marked BUILDING GUIDE. He flipped through the pages to find each floor was labeled. Like Dante's Hell, each level was reserved for specific perverts. Nothing for the first floor except a gym and a shower room. The second floor was for fecal fetishists. There was a room for people who wanted to shit down the throats of kidnapped nuns.

The fourth floor was for bestiality. There was no seventh floor. The tenth was for those who wanted to torture animals of all kinds. A room was labeled ENDANGERED SPECIES. There was also a dinosaur room for people who wanted to masturbate on fossils.

The thirteenth floor was for rapists. The fourteenth was for child-fuckers. The twenty-first was for orgies where only five of a twenty-minimum party were willing participants.

The thirtieth floor was for serial killers. The thirty-sixth was for cannibals. The thirty-ninth was for necrophiles.

The more he read, the faster he flipped through the laminated pages. Finally, after seeing that the forty-fifth floor was for skull-fucking people that resembled Jesus Christ, he skipped to the end.

The ninety-second floor. The penthouse. Labeled simply, THE MASTER. According to the text, a security key and a special pass were required to gain access to this floor.

George went to the unconscious guard and stole his key ring. It was a heavy, jangling creature of many limbs. Thankfully, he found each key was labeled with a small circular sticker with abbreviations written on each one. PENTH could only mean one thing.

He opened the drawers until he found a file folder filled with security passes. Most of them were the regular kind, but the very last one was labeled MASTER-PENTH. He clipped it to his belt.

Gripping the gun in one hand, George marched to the elevator, his mouth set grim and deep in his face, nearly as deep as his hollowed, murderous eyes. He pressed the UP arrow with the barrel of the .38, and the doors dinged and opened at once.

It was a well-lit box into which he stepped. Everything sparkled cleanly, even the buttons, which showed no sign of wear. The button at the top was labeled 35. He pressed the button.

The trip was short, a lot shorter than he'd expected, and he had to pop his ears more than once. Though he knew there was certainly going to be violence ahead of him, he felt nothing but a slight tension. Still, a more sensible part of his mind tried to convince him to turn back.

*Face facts, George. You can't* Die Hard *this place. This isn't a movie, and you're no star. You're an accountant. Leave. Get the police.*

Except, his family might be dead by then. He didn't like the idea of the Master wearing his wife, or maybe even his son, as a condom.

*Ding!* The doors opened, and George stepped out. He stood in a corridor, and saw plenty of doors up and down the walls. It was very decorative, but there were a lot of blood stains on the carpets and red streaks everywhere, even on the ceiling. Sledgehammers were all over the place: on flower tables, leaning against walls, even hanging from hooks. Many of them were tinted crimson.

One of the doors opened, and out stepped a clean-cut, well-dressed man with a thick mop of slicked back hair. In his slender hands, he held a baby, and he cooed at it. The baby gurgled happily.

"Um, excuse me sir," George said.

The man held up a finger—please hold a moment—and placed the baby gently on the floor.

"Shit, don't do that. Have you seen how nasty this place looks?"

Again, the man held his finger up. Casually, he strolled over to a sledgehammer leaning up against the wall. He tested the weight of it. Then, he approached the baby, and it dawned on George what was going to happen.

"Put the fucking sledgehammer down."

"Of course," the man said.

George brought up the guard's gun, but he was too late. The man didn't theatrically hold up the sledgehammer before bringing it down. Like an animal, he snarled and jabbed it down at the baby. There was no yelp from the infant; its little baby head exploded under the weight of the hammer's head.

George's gun barked, and the baby-basher went down, blood gouting from the top of his shattered head. George wanted to fire again, but he took another look at the baby-basher and saw that the scumbag looked as dead as the baby.

"Motherfucker," he said.

He looked around and behind him, where he discovered another elevator. This one had one button: UP. With one final look at the baby-basher's twitching body, he pressed the UP button.

After a moment, the doors dinged and opened, but this time someone stepped out, a middle-aged paunchy man with very little hair and a small pair of spectacles perched on his bulbous nose. His forehead shone with sweat, but his clothes were immaculate. Under one arm, he held what appeared to be the skull of a small dinosaur. The eyeholes gleamed wetly.

This new stranger saw the dead body behind George. He saw the smoking gun. And then he saw the badge clipped to George's belt.

"My goodness! How much did you pay for that?" Pointing at George's waist. "I pay through the nose just to masturbate on dinosaurs. I can't imagine what shooting someone must cost. Still, I can dream, right? I just came from the seventieth floor. You should see what they pay for up there. Wow!"

George brought the gun up and aimed it at the newcomer.

"Whoa! Easy, tiger. Your business is your business. I shouldn't have asked."

George pulled the trigger, and the fossil-fucker's nose disappeared in a crimson cloud. The dinosaur skull dropped from his grip and rolled away, next to the dead baby. The body twitched for a moment before dropping to the stained carpet, still.

George didn't bother to look down at his latest kill. Instead, he stepped over the body and entered the elevator.

This time, the buttons ranged from 36 to 70. George didn't take the time to consider, he merely pressed the 70 button. The doors closed, and the elevator whooshed up. Before long, the number over the door became 70, and the door slid open. George stalked out of the elevator, gripping the gun tightly.

George found himself in yet another corridor, but there were no sledgehammers to be found here. Instead, knives and cleavers and other sharp instruments were strewn about everywhere. Like the other floor, there were a lot of bloodstains on the carpets, but it looked like they were mixing with a few other bodily fluids.

There were a couple of women standing nearby, both dressed in skimpy evening dresses. Both struck him as incredibly beautiful, and they smoked from long, slender black cigarette holders. They wore fashionable gloves up to their elbows. One looked like she was in her mid-fifties, and the other had to be in her early-twenties. They looked a lot alike, as if they were mother and daughter. Both stopped talking as soon as they saw George. They glanced at the pass on his belt.

"My!" the older one said. "Look what management sent us!"

"Isn't he adorable?" the other said.

Both approached him and started running their fingers through his thinning hair. He was too stunned to do anything about it. How long had it been since a beautiful woman had touched him? Probably when Ellen was younger. She'd been good-looking then. Now, she was short and stout like many middle-aged women. Not much to recommend her.

"Look at you," the older one said. "You look like a real person with hair like that."

"He's so old. He must have just come from the suburbs."

George cleared his throat. "I *am* from the suburbs."

"It talks!" the older one said.

"Mommy! I want to see his cock!"

"Um. Excuse me?" George swallowed hard enough to hear it in his own head.

"You heard my daughter. She wants to see your penis. Remove your pants at once."

"Uh . . . no."

"We're paying good money for this! I demand to see your cock!"

George remembered the gun, and he brought it up, aiming it at the mother's face. The woman flinched and backed away.

"Don't worry, Mommy. He just needs to relax a bit."

She reached to the straps of her dress, and with a couple of deft twists, the dress fell away, revealing her sleek, nubile body. George's eyes went wide, and he tried not to look, but his eyes traveled down to her perky breasts, both of which stared him down. His eyes drifted further down her body until they found the landing strip of her pubic hair. The cleft of her vagina looked tight and inviting.

George's gun lowered slightly, and he breathed heavily through his mouth.

"Yes," the mother said. "My daughter's quite beautiful. Her pussy tastes like ambrosia. You should consider eating my little darling out . . . but not before seeing how superior her mother is first."

The mother's dress fell away. Her body was not fresh like her daughter's, but it was still gorgeous. The fine wine of age had turned her into a curvy goddess. Her breasts were heavy, but perfectly round. She had stayed in shape. There was no pubic hair on her, just smooth, rounded flesh above a pair of bubble gum lips.

The gun now hung by George's side so loosely it felt like he was about to drop it. He all but panted at this point, and he didn't know which woman he wanted to watch more as his eyes darted from daughter to mother and then back again.

"Can I play with him, Mommy? Oh, can I?"

"Of course, sweetheart."

The daughter grinned. "Come with me."

She took his hand and he followed behind her, zombie-like, as they walked into one of the myriad rooms down this hallway.

George found himself in a gorgeous room decorated mostly red. A large king-sized, four-poster bed with velvet and silk sheets and a canopy dominated the room, and the velvet curtains concealed the world outside the skyscraper. It looked beautiful at first, but as he got a closer look, he would realized that the amazing decoration was crusted brown with dried blood.

The daughter led George toward the bed. He didn't notice the table to his right and against the wall. There were blood-stained cutting tools and a line of desiccated meat on the surface. Severed penises.

But he walked by without noticing them. He was too busy looking at the young woman's perfect peach of an ass, bouncing back and forth with her stride.

Finally they stopped, and the mother massaged George's shoulders. The daughter turned and sat down on her bed, looking up into George's eyes with a coy smile.

"I hope you have a big cock," the daughter said. "It's been a long time since I've had a thick, juicy cock."

George couldn't say anything. The woman in front of him was one of the most beautiful women he'd ever seen, and she clearly wanted him more than anything else. He watched her hands go to his belt buckle. There was a clatter as it came undone, and a snapping sound as she unclasped his button. The zipper went down, and his pants fell away, revealing boxers.

He didn't stop her as she pulled at the waistband of his shorts and eased them down. He wasn't huge, but he wasn't small, either. Most importantly, he was semi-hard. The gun hung by his side, forgotten, and he nearly drooled all over this woman.

The young woman made cooing sounds as she grabbed a hold of him. The mother peered over George's shoulder and saw his raging erection about to disappear into her daughter's mouth. "She really likes you. She doesn't do that for just anyone."

The mother slowly took the gun from George's hand and set it aside, out of his reach. She then kissed George. He didn't kiss her back, and he was too stunned to stop her.

"I think he's all ready for you, Mommy."

The mother fell back onto the bed and spread her legs. The daughter slipped aside and pulled George forward by his dick. She aimed him for her mother's pussy.

Just before their genitals connected, George paused. Guilt finally got the better of him. Who knew what was happening to his family, and here he was, about to get his rocks off? "Jesus. What am I doing? I can't do this." But he didn't pull back. He stared down at the inch of space between his dick and her pussy.

"I'm a married man. I can't do this."

"Married men do this all the time," the mother said.

"No. My family." He shook his head, suddenly realizing the sheer insanity of this moment. "I have to save my family."

As he pulled back, he tripped over his pants and boxers, which were still around his ankles. He fell to the floor, and the daughter jumped onto him, pressing her naked ass against his face. With the one hand, she grabbed George's purple, thick-veined hard-on. She brought a box cutter—-where the fuck did that come from?--to the base of his cock and was about to cut when her mother intervened.

"No, honey. You know how I like it."

"What the fuck are you doing?!" George screamed. He managed to turn his head to the side so he no longer tasted her anus on his mouth.

"He won't want to do it, Mommy. Just let me cut it off."

"I'm your mother. Do as you're told."

With an exasperated sigh, the daughter rolled away, and George scuttered backward. He saw the box cutter, and he tried to cover up his erection. It was too big to hide.

"Can I say, Mommy? Can I?"

"Sure, sweetheart."

"You're going to fuck Mommy as hard as you can. And then, just when you're about to cum, I'm going to sneak between your legs and cut your cock off. Then, the real fun begins."

George couldn't believe what she'd said.

"Then, while you're busy screaming and crying, I'm going to go down on Mommy and suck your dick out of her. And I'm going to drink blood from your wilting cock."

"And we'll save it for our collection," her mother finished.

"What the fuck?" George said.

The daughter strode over to the table and plucked up a severed penis. She tossed it to George, where it bounced off his chest and landed on the floor. He looked down at it, and his eyes went wide. It resembled a piece of beef jerky.

"Now get over here and fuck me so my daughter can cut your dick off."

"Fuck you!" George yelled.

The mother held up his gun and pointed it at him. "Get

over here now, or I'll make it hurt for a long time."

George looked down at himself and was surprised to see that he was still as hard as an iron bar. There was a tiny nick at the base where the daughter was about to cut, and a tiny spot of blood had risen.

The daughter brandished her blade, and George glanced at the gun in the mother's hand. Slowly, he stood and stopped bothering to cover himself up. He climbed up on the bed and slid up toward the mother. The daughter stood behind him, licking her lips as she fingered the blade.

George grabbed his dick and squeezed until it was so hard it felt like it was going to explode. Then, just as he was about to ease into her, he started to convulse and groan.

"What are you--?" the mother said.

George came so hard that ropes of semen traveled all the way up to the mother's neck. To get it all out, he kept stroking himself until he was finally out of juice and he looked strained.

"Sorry," he said, panting. "I'm only good for one go. You'll have to finish without me."

She grabbed his cock and pulled. Hard. "You're still erect. Put it in me. Now."

George's face wilted as he realized his premature ejaculation plan had fallen through. She pulled him toward her until he was about to enter her.

The door suddenly opened, and in stepped a slender, frail looking youth. He looked so much like the other two, he could only be the daughter's brother. He was naked, and his tiny penis poked out of his thick pubic hair like a badger peering out of a bush. In one of his hands, he held a freshly severed penis, and he sucked the blood from the raw, open end.

George saw his chance. While the castration family was distracted, he went for the gun and easily pried it from the mother's hand.

"No!" she cried.

"What's going on?" her son asked.

George turned the gun on the mother's face and without thinking twice, he fired a bullet between her eyes. Her brains blew out the back of her head, and blood poured out from the hole in her face, drenching her naked body in shiny red.

The daughter snarled and jabbed the box cutter into George's right buttock, nearly lopping it in half. George screamed as he fell forward, one hand on his ass. He tried to roll, but the daughter was on him and sliced into his back.

"You killed my mother! I'll kill you! I'll fucking kill you!"

George screamed as his blood flew everywhere. Before she could make a second cut, his fear gave him the strength to push off the floor, knocking her off of him. She skidded across the carpet, and the box cutter flew away.

This didn't stop her. Rage propelled her up, snarling and ready to bite and claw her way to revenge.

George did the only thing he could think to do: he aimed the gun and pulled the trigger, but fear threw off his aim. Instead of plugging her between the eyes, he blew off her jaw. Blood rained down on her tits, and her tongue lolled out of the gaping raw hole. She began to choke on her own blood.

The daughter dropped the severed penis and stared at George. They watched each other for what seemed like forever before the son started inching toward a cleaver on the table.

"Don't do it," George said.

The son paid him no heed. He swept up the cleaver and stared into George's eyes. He got a good grip and then seemed like he was about to jump forward.

He took one step, and George shot him in the chest, driving the blood and soul out of him in one easy step.

The frail young man fell first to his knees and then onto his face, dead like the rest of his family.

George looked down at himself and saw that he as finally flaccid again. The pain and fear finally released that tension.

He bent down to pull up his pants when he felt a sudden jolt of pain, and he grimaced. He reached behind him and touched his laid open buttock. His fingers came back red. There was more blood from the wound on his back.

George looked around and saw another door in here. He could see it led to a bathroom. He shuffled over to the door. Inside, George turned his back to the mirror so he could see how bad the damage was. The blood slowed to a slight ooze, but he could tell the wounds were deep. He'd need stitches.

And then, an odd grin came across his face. *Bruce Willis has nothing up on me.*

He turned around and started rummaging through the medicine cabinet. The only drugs he found here were little blue Viagra pills with the occasional tablet of ecstasy.

He fared better under the sink. Here he found a bottle of hydrogen peroxide. Lifting up his shirt, he poured the bottle over his wound. It bubbled, and he gritted his teeth. Next, he poured it on his wounded buttock, and this time he bit his lip hard enough to draw blood.

After a moment, he was satisfied that this was the best he could do for now. He stooped to gingerly pull his pants up. The last thing he did was check the gun.

One bullet left. Fuck.

It would have to do. He snapped the gun shut and went back into the castration family's room. He did not favor their corpses with so much as a glance as he went back to the corridor and found the next elevator that would lead him to his destination.

This time, the numbers went from seventy-one to

ninety-one. There was also a button simply labeled P, and it had a keyhole next to it. He flipped through the guard's keys until he found the right one and slid it home. He turned it and pressed the P button. It lit up, and he sailed up to the very top of the skyscraper.

He stepped out and saw that all that remained was to pass through a set of double doors. A sensor and keypad jutted from the wall by the doors.

*Keypad?* he thought. *Shit.* The booklet hadn't mentioned this, and there was no way he could crack it.

He looked at the pass, as if that would offer a clue. Surprisingly enough, it did more that that. Written in the smallest script he'd ever seen were three numbers.

He groaned inwardly, almost insulted by the combination. With a shake of his head, he held the pass up to the sensor, and when it beeped, he punched the same number three times. There was a click, and he opened one door slowly.

George slipped in quietly, pointing the gun first left, then right in imitation of every cop show he'd ever seen. No one in sight, not so much as a guard. Music softly caressed his ear. *Mozart?* he wondered. He'd never heard anything of Mozart's before, but it sounded too classy to have been composed by anyone else.

He eased his way down the hallway, stopping to look into the kitchen. Holding the gun before him like a vampire hunter would a cross, he stepped in. The counter was loaded with utensils and pans, as if someone was getting ready to cook something.

*My arm,* he thought, and shuddered.

Steam chugged from a pot on the stove like smoke from a chimney. Though he suspected it would be a bad idea, he had to know what was cooking. Steeling his stomach for whatever he might find, he approached the pot and looked in.

It appeared to be fish, and they moved around as if they were still alive. It took him a moment to recognize the cashew-like hump, and he nearly gagged, backing away from the fetus stew.

*How can they do this?* his twisting, contorted mind begged. *It's too much! Too fucking much!* But listening to Mozart drifting from the next room, he thought he had an idea as to the answer.

George followed the music, the gun a proboscis, and when he found the source, he nearly doubled over with sickness.

There was a long dining table with only one chair, which was situated at the far end. In it sat a man dressed in a neat Armani suit and tie. He was slender and middle-aged with a full head of silver hair slicked back. Propped in his right eye was a gold-rimmed monocle. He smoked a cigarette jutting from a slim black holder clenched in his perfect white teeth. He was strikingly handsome and could have passed for a Hollywood star, if not for the rest of the room.

Trussed up and naked in front of him was a young boy, maybe seventeen. His legs were tied up and pulled above his head, and the man's head was between the kid's legs, sniffing like a dog.

It took George a moment to recognize the kid as Jordan.

Two other figures stood nearby. One was a towering, muscular bald man, and he held a gun on the other person, who turned out to be Ellen. She was naked, sort of. She wore what George originally thought was a costume. Of course, in this place, nothing was fake. No, she was wearing the skin of a well-toned man, sans the head. The chest had been cut out to allow her meaty, stretch-marked breasts to hang out. Her own hands also poked out at the skin's wrists, and they both massaged the flaccid genitals of the previous owner. Ellen stared at the man who could only be the Master, no emotion showing, as if she were beyond illness. George wondered what she'd been forced to see—-to do—-that would make her seem so dead.

"Your anus smells . . . superb," the Master said in a cultured voice. "I'm tempted to eat it raw." He looked to Ellen, perhaps seeking a response. "Please, Ellen, masturbate faster."

Ellen's hands worked the dead penis faster. She didn't respond in any other way.

"I think I shall have you for supper tomorrow," the Master said to Jordan. He gave the boy's buttock a sharp slap. Jordan screamed through his gag, eyes wide.

"No, no!" The Master laughed. "Not all of you! I'm going to have Javier core out your asshole, and then your mother will prepare it for me while I watch you bleed to death. Perhaps I'll let you have a bite of my meal, if you last that long."

He paused, rubbing his chin as if he were contemplating the meaning of life. "Where is the arm? Javier, be a dear and get on the walkie talkie. Find out, would you?"

The man behind Ellen holstered his gun under his arm and reached for his walkie talkie. George took his chance; before Javier could press the button on the side, George stepped up to him and put the remaining bullet into his bald head, spreading his brains on the wall behind him like a painter's accident. Ellen jumped at the sudden sound, but she said nothing. She didn't even scream as she collapsed, sprayed with pieces of Javier.

George couldn't spare the time to check on her; the Master was already up and armed with a knife. He'd drawn his arm back, as if he were about to throw the blade. "Freeze!" he shouted, like a clichéd TV cop.

The Master ignored him and threw the knife. Startled, George pulled the trigger, even though he knew the gun was empty. He couldn't get out of the path of the blade.

Luckily, the Master didn't have very good aim. Instead of hitting anything vital, the knife went into George's shoulder. Either he was finally getting used to being cut up, or he was in shock. He barely noticed as he lunges at the Master.

The Master jabbed the fork at George's eye, but got his cheek instead. The prongs sank halfway into his skin, but George was so full of rage he didn't notice. Instead, he brought the gun down like a club on the top of the Master's head. The gray hair split, and red started oozing down his forehead.

George didn't stop. He continued to club the Master with the gun, even as the Master fell to the ground, his face a horrible red, gushing pulp. Now kneeling over him, George pounded away, letting loose a series of growls and curses as he brutally reduced the Master's head to a chunky pancake. Blood stained the white carpet, and it splattered George's face and forearms.

Finally, he started to tire, and the beat of his assault slowed until he couldn't lift the gun to hit him again. That was when he noticed the fork and yanked it out of his face. He looked at the blood on the prongs, then shrugged and dropped it.

Out of breath, he pushed himself to his feet and stared down at the mess he'd caused. Absently, he reached for the steak knife in his arm and pulled it out. He grimaced a little when he did this, but pain was still far and away for him.

Finally, he tore his eyes away from the Master's corpse and turned to see Jordan. The boy tried to get his father's attention by waving his bound hands and grunting loudly.

George approached Jordan and, like a robot, he cut his son's bonds away.

As soon as the gag was gone, Jordan cried out, "Dad! Oh thank God!" He said more, but the words were lost in his hysterical sobs.

George grabbed him by his skinny upper arms and shook him. "Jordan! Quick! Where's your brother? Where's Denny?"

Jordan stopped crying and sniffled. "I . . . that is . . .

he . . . ." He pointed a quivering finger at the Master, sprawled on the floor like an overturned bowl of pasta.

"Go on," George said. "What about the Master?"

"He said . . . he said . . . ."

"Denny's dead," Ellen said from behind him. He turned to see her sitting up, still dressed in a dead man's flesh. She struggled her way out of it.

"How?" he managed to croak.

"I don't know," she said. "The . . . this man just told us he'd had Denny killed."

George was aghast at this. "Then, he could still be alive! We have to find him! We--!"

"HE'S DEAD!" Ellen's strained face had gone red, and she gagged, trying to keep her composure. She pushed herself to her feet and said, "Don't you get it? These people, they do whatever they want. Why would they lie to us? They probably threw him to those animals on the fourteenth floor."

George could no longer look her in the eye. He turned to Jordan, who was now wrapped in a towel he'd found in the bathroom. His son offered an identical towel to Ellen.

"Can we go, Dad? Please?" Jordan's voice was flat and tremulous. He looked at the floor when he spoke.

This shook George out of thoughts of Denny. One son was probably dead, but the other was definitely alive, and he wanted to keep it that way. He dropped the knife and grabbed his wife's hand on his left side and his son's on the right. The family walked as one toward the door. When they opened it, George said, "I'm not giving up on Denny. We're going to the police, and—-"

"Of course you'll go to the police," a British voice said, and George pulled everyone to a halt.

Standing between them and the elevator was a group of twelve camo-ed and ski-masked men, six kneeling and six above them, aiming assault weapons at the family. Behind them stood a thirteenth man, dressed in a camo suit like the others, but no ski mask obscured his features.

His blond hair was ruffled, and he smiled as he lounged against the wall, arms crossed.

"You must go to the police," he said, blue eyes twinkling. "You'll have to explain how things have gotten to this point. However, I think you should show discretion in what you say. Remember, Mr. Penderghast, you killed several people today."

"You're not going to let us go," George said. "We killed the Master. We know too much."

The man burst into laughter. When he managed to calm down, he said, "That wasn't the Master. Do you seriously believe the Master exists? Did Uncle Sam ever exist? Or Lady Liberty? No, the Master's just a symbol. You killed one of our highest paying perverts, but he'd been on credit for the last few months. His tastes were too expensive, and he could no longer afford us. We'll miss him, but quality service has its cost. So, of course you're free to go. You can't cause us trouble. We have too much money."

"I'm not leaving without my son," George said.

"I thought you'd say that." The man reached behind him and grabbed a Ziploc bag full of red-tinted mush. He threw it to the floor at George's feet, where it burst open and washed over his shoes. The only recognizable thing in the mess was an eyeball. Brown, just like Denny's.

"You will leave," the man said. "Go to the police, as I know you must, but mind what you say. This is a warning, not a threat, and it's for your own good. Remember Orpheus on his way out of the Underworld."

George heard none of this. Rage built up in his heart and burned its course to the top of his head, where it seemed to ignite his brain. He started forward, his fists raised, but Ellen and Jordan held him back.

"Don't!" Ellen said. "Please. Remember the last time you didn't listen to me?"

*If only I had listened,* he thought. *We'd be safe. Hell, we'd probably be on our way home by now.* George looked down at the slop on the floor. At the eyeball. The hands of his family felt greasy on his arms, but he knew he couldn't put them in any further danger. If it was just him, he wouldn't have cared about his own life, but his wife and Jordan were still alive. He let his fists drop.

"If you're really going to let us go," George said, "step aside."

The man grinned, showing off the teeth of an angel, just as white as his own skin, and spread his arms out, as if he expected a hug. "You heard him. Step aside."

The men standing moved to the right side of the hall, and those kneeling went to the left. The man joined the latter.

George pulled his family after him. As they passed between the pillars of armed men, his stomach turned to rubber as he expected them to close in on them and kill them anyway. None of the masked men so much as twitched.

The man opened the elevator doors for them. "Take care, Mr. Penderghast."

The three of them stepped into the elevator, but just before George could push the GF button, the man said, "Oh, there's one more thing!"

*Shit,* George thought. *Here it comes.*

His belly tightened as he expected a hail of bullets to tear them to pieces, but the man simply reached to George's belt and grabbed the security pass. "Thank *you,* sir," the man said. "Have a good day."

George stabbed the button with his finger, and he didn't loosen up until the doors closed, banishing the man from his sight.

### 8

True to the man's word, no one prevented them from leaving, not even at the glass door. They halted long enough to breathe in the fresh air, and they didn't stop again until they found a phone and called the police.

George spoke for them all, and no one contradicted him when he told the detective that they'd been robbed by a bunch of kids, and their car had been stolen. The kids had guns, and they made Ellen and Jordan undress, just for laughs. They then kidnapped Denny and ran away. He'd tried to stop them, but one of them stabbed him several times.

The police reassured them that everything would be done to find their son. The detective offered his card, in case they needed anything in the future.

Of course, the police found nothing. Denny was declared dead after a year. Jordan never spoke a word again in his life, and he spent a good deal of time in a vegetative state. George started drinking heavily, and he never went back to work again. Only Ellen managed to keep it together, although she was more like a zombie than anything else.

George made it for another year before the truth gnawed his guts away. He knew his family would object, so he told them he was going out for another bottle of Jim Beam. He left them a note, but that was it.

He went to the police, to the detective who had taken his statement. This time, he told the detective what had really happened, and George Penderghast was never seen again, except by the denizens of the thirteenth floor of a particular skyscraper.

Ellen found the note, and when her husband didn't come home, she knew what had happened and understood how the monsters in the skyscraper continued to get away with their crimes.

She took Jordan and moved out to the country, where they went weeks without human contact, which was just the way she wanted it.

## 9

They watched the station wagon approach. The light was on, and the woman in the passenger seat was looking at a map. The man who was driving looked left and right, squinting to read the street signs. In the back was a baby in a safety seat, crying its little eyes out.

The kids raised their rocks and bottles and started to throw them at the car. It screeched to a halt, and the man got out.

"You sons of bitches!" he roared. "What do you think you're doing?!"

Denny Penderghast smiled, raising his slingshot as his companions drew together, waiting for the rumble to begin.

# STORY NOTES

**AMBER:** People are divided by this one. They either love it or hate it. It was something I'd written to break my usual style, and I thought I'd see if I could pull off a story in almost exclusively a figurative fashion. I get a kick out of it even today, but some people still look for an explanation. It's a neat little tale, and I learned a few new tricks from it. Without this one, I wouldn't have been able to write some of my more popular pieces later on.

**RIDING THE MIDNIGHT GLOOM:** I know more junkies than I care to. I almost became one, myself, when I had some health issues that only Dilaudid could help me with. I know what opiates are capable of, so when several junkies started telling me that shooting up sometimes leads to out of body experiences, I was surprised (and pretty skeptical). After a while, I decided that they were probably talking about it in a metaphorical sense, but what if they weren't? This story came from that little seed of an idea. On a side note, this tale has a special place in my heart. Not only did it place in a contest run by the Horror Library (judged by Fran Friel), it also found publication in LIQUID IMAGINATION. The fine folks over there adapted it for an audio book, my first and only such publication. The guy they got to read it even pronounced my last name right without consulting me, something that is apparently harder than it seems. (Brun-ee, not Brun-eye.)

**VIRTUOSO:** This comes from a very strange period of my life. I was just starting to get into bizarro fiction, and I was listening to a lot of Jerry Cantrell back then. This story just evolved from that odd mixture brewing in my head. I know it's not batshit crazy enough to qualify as actual bizarro, but it's pretty far out there. This one is one of my favorites.

**SUICIDAL TENDENCIES:** This one has a long fuckin' history, folks. It was inspired by reading a lot of Kurt Vonnegut and Chuck Palahniuk. Granted, by the time I wrote this one, the horror structure was pretty old (usually, it was dedicated to hitchhiker stories; you know the kind, a driver picks up a hitchhiker, and it turns out both guys are serial killers with the intent of killing each other), but I thought I brought something new to it. Technically, neither of my characters are serial killers. They just have a history of driving others to commit suicide. But the thing was, and I thought I was sooooo clever back then, neither of my main characters would wind up killing each other in the end. In the original finale, the leader of their group therapy wound up snapping and murdering everyone in the room, including the two "serial killers."

Wow. That's pretty good evidence that I didn't know how to structure a story back then. Regardless, I showed it to a very close friend of mine (and on-again-off-again girlfriend; don't ask, long story), Nicole Evans, and she decided she knew how to fix things. She added considerably to the story, and much to my pleasure, one of the hottest up-and-coming horror fiction magazines of the time bought it for publication.

Well, they paid on publication, so we never saw money for it. Too bad, considering how things turned out. (I'm not going to mention the title of the magazine—-I'm too classy for that [collar pull]--but I'm sure a few of you out there can figure out which one it was.) Sadly, the original publisher sold the magazine. Luckily, the new publisher decided he liked our story enough to keep it on their publishing schedule.

Before long, he stopped returning my emails. It became very apparent that something was wrong, and after doing a lot of research, I discovered that the magazine had gone out of business before publishing the story. The fellas in charge over there didn't have the courtesy to tell me that they wouldn't be publishing our story. Too bad. Once upon a time, I was an editor of a magazine, and I would have certainly told my contributors if I wouldn't be able to publish their work. As a result of this fuck up, I lost months of time in getting this one out there. We finally sold it to THE MONSTERS NEXT DOOR, an excellent online magazine, so this one has a happy ending, but what a fucking ordeal.

**FAMILY MAN:** I'm really proud of this story. It made the rounds, and generally, editors seemed to like it. They just thought the ending was too goofy for them. That was, indeed, the effect I was going for. I needed absurdity and violence, and I think I pulled it off. It convinced at least one editor to print it; as a result, it made it into Pill Hill's anthology, A HACKED-UP HOLIDAY MASSACRE. I was in there with titans like Jack Ketchum, Wrath James White, and Nate Southard, but I'm most thrilled by the fact that I wound up following a reprint of a story by my absolute favorite writer of all time, Joe R. Lansdale. How could I fail with a lead in like "By Bizarre Hands?"

**PIMP OF THE LIVING DEAD:** This is the story that prompted me to start publishing TABARD INN: TALES

OF QUESTIONABLE TASTE. It was one of the ugliest, most horrifying stories I'd written, and I could only send it to a handful of places. Back then, magazines weren't accepting material like this, and as a result, it wasn't considered by many editors. I wanted to have a magazine where this kind of thing wasn't just tolerated, it was accepted with open arms. I didn't put it in the first or second issue, though. I waited until the third, and I published it under a pen name, mostly because I felt guilty about publishing something of my own. It's kind of a dick-ish thing to do, so I lied to everyone and said this story was written by a sick bastard in prison. Now the truth can be told. Sorry.

**CORPUSPLASTY:** There isn't much to this story. When I write flash fiction, I'm usually in a playful mood. I think that's a habit heavily influenced by my favorite writer (did I mention that yet?), Joe R. Lansdale.

**A PLACE TO BE:** The campground is a real place. I encountered it when I was a younger, drunker man, and seeing all of those signs about the vets of our wars inspired this story directly. I was also feeling pretty maudlin back in those days, looking for a place of my own to be. I haven't found it yet, but that doesn't mean I've stopped looking.

**THE SPACE IN THE BOTTOM OF MARTIN OGLESBY'S DESK DRAWER:** Who hasn't worked in an office? I currently work in one, and while I might have exaggerated a few things, the heart of this story remains the same.

**SHRINK:** As you can imagine, this one came from a very angry part of my life. I'm a firm believer in the need for fury. There's a reason it's one of our human ingredients, even though our society seems intent on suppressing it whenever it can. I think that's pretty dangerous, and I'm sure the protagonist of this story would agree.

**TIMELY:** I'm always in a hurry, and I drive like a fucking maniac. Every day I go in to work, I'm blazing down I-290 at about ninety miles-per-hour. One day, while I was in the fast lane doing just this, I noticed a state trooper nearby. I slowed down to the prescribed 55, and he pulled into the fast lane behind me. Nervously, I watched him in the rearview mirror, wondering if he'd seen how fast I was going. Then, to my dismay, as I was running a bit late that day, he pulled me over. Not for speeding, no: for NOT speeding. I was in the fast lane, and I wasn't going fast enough for him. I wanted to tell the motherfucker that I would have been speeding if not for him, but seeing as how I wanted to get out of a ticket, I remained polite. I was given a warning for that incident, and me wishing for him to go away and let me get to work on time eventually led to the writing of this story.

**BASEBALL PLAYERS ARE A SUPERSTITIOUS LOT:** Blame Shirley Jackson's "The Lottery" for this one. I thought I'd write a parody of her story back in college, and everyone seemed to think it was pretty funny. Fast forward years later, to when I got a job selling ad space at Central Newspaper. I was really lousy at that job (I only lasted two weeks at it), but my boss wanted to run fiction in his papers. I mentioned that I'm a writer, and he asked to see a few things. He also published a couple other stories (that don't appear here, because they're really not that great), but when it came to this one, he called me up maybe three months after he'd fired me. He told me the publisher didn't want to print it because it depicted violence against women. I had to explain that it's not a serious story, that it's a parody of one of the most widely read stories ever written. He went to the publisher with this new information, and she changed her mind and printed it.

**SLUMMIN' IT:** This is another of my more popular

stories, and when people look for a sample of my work, I usually offer this one up to them. It came from the idea that a masochistic dilettante would never, ever want to do truly nasty things to themselves. However, if they figured out a way to inhabit someone else's body, they'd be free to commit all sorts of vile acts unto themselves. All the pain, none of the cost.

A NIGHT IN THE UNLIFE: Just like I can't write an ordinary zombie story, I can't write an ordinary vampire story. What if vampires were regular people, and human beings were the monsters? That's the thought that birthed this tale. At first, it had a much weaker ending, but thanks to the folks over at NIGHT TO DAWN, where it was originally published, I was able to change it to something a lot more satisfying. You don't even want to see the original, lame ending. Trust me.

YUM: This is another story that originally had a shitty ending. Yet again, I'm glad I rewrote it, because it's a pretty nifty idea, and it would have been horrible to waste. It should be noted that this is the oldest story in this collection. When I first wrote it, I'd been reading a lot of mysteries. I wanted to get my own series detective out there, and Cameron Laurich was my guy. He appeared in several unpublished novels and a few short stories (one of which showed up in DETECTIVE MYSTERY STORIES, a story called "Free Garbage Day"), all of which is so terrible that none of it will ever see the light of day. It's too bad. He's an okay guy. Maybe someday, he'll have his moment. For now, he'll have to settle for "Yum."

OUTSIDE HER WINDOW, IT WAITS: This is a story inspired by my co-writer on "Suicidal Tendencies." Nicole really did draw the picture in question, and she does, indeed, have a strange way of holding a cigarette, but rest assured, the rest of the character didn't really come from her. The story about the hand is also true, but that one is from my childhood. Anyway, back when I was editing TABARD INN, a particular writer would submit stories to me that were good, but they weren't the kind of thing I was looking for. After a while, I saw that she'd become an editor in her own right, and I decided to give her the chance to reject me by sending her this story. She even said in her response that she looked forward to shooting me down. Instead, she bought the story for an anthology. I'm proud of that, and to this day, I wish I could have published something of hers.

**MONSTER COCK:** As I'm sure you can imagine, no one was interested in publishing this one. It's based on a dream I had in which I grew up to the size of a giant and fucked the sun. The image was too good for me to pass up, so I put it down to paper and steeled myself for the inevitable rejection letters. Shortly after, I hung out with Jon Michael Lennon of CheeseLord Comics, and Leo Perez, who was just starting his long association with Jon. I thought they might want to adapt it for an issue of PRODUCT OF SOCIETY (they eventually published an adaptation of a non-fiction story from me), and much to my delight, Leo started drawing a picture of a giant cock on the spot. We were at a Denny's, and he just whipped out his sketch book and went to town. I couldn't stop laughing. I desperately hoped a waitress would notice and mention something, but sadly that did not happen.

**THE SKYSCRAPER OF FORBIDDEN DELIGHT:** The idea for this story was sparked by a real incident. A friend told me that she had been driving waaaaaay out in the country, and her car had been assaulted by a pack of kids throwing rocks and bottles and just about everything they could at her. She was urged by her passenger to drive away and fast. She was later told that if they'd stopped, the kids would have robbed them, as that is a common practice out in that area.

I joined that with an idea that I've always had about isolation. Why do horror stories always happen out in the middle of nowhere? There are places in heavily inhabited cities that are just as isolated. And do villains always have to be rednecks? Why not rich people? I decided to apply my friend's real life story to this idea. All I needed was a suitable bad guy, and the only one who could pull it off is someone who is extravagantly rich. Surprise! I had my theme. This is another one that had no chance in hell of getting published in a magazine or anthology. I'm proud to present it here for the first time.

# About the Author

John Bruni's work has appeared in a variety of anthologies, most notably in VILE THINGS from Comet Press, A HACKED-UP HOLIDAY MASSACRE from Pill Hill, and ZOMBIE! ZOMBIE! BRAIN BANG! from StrangeHouse Books. His stories have also been published in SHROUD, CTHULHU SEX, MORPHEUS TALES, and a number of other magazines. He was the editor of TABARD INN: TALES OF QUESTIONABLE TASTE, and he is the author of a crime novel, STRIP, from Musa Publishing. Check out his website at talesofquestionabletaste.com, his blog at talesofunspeakabletaste.blogspot.com, and follow him on Twitter at @tusitalabruni, if you have the testicular fortitude. He lives, drinks, and fucks in Elmhurst, IL

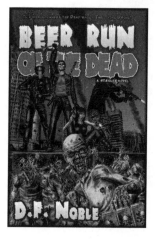
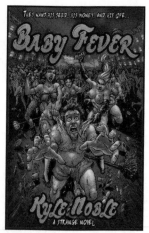

*"WHERE THE WEIRD, THE HORRIFIC, AND THE BIZARRE MEET THE STRANGE"*

## "Cannibal Fat Camp"
### Mark Scioneaux
### David C. Hayes

Miles Landish can't help himself. He eats and eats and eats and eats just to fill an empty, gaping, hole in his self esteem. Nothing ever seems to fill that hole, even the five star meals Miles' wealthy parents make possible. So, as a last resort, Miles attends Camp Tum Tum, a weight control camp for spoiled teens. What happens there is only hinted at in high social circles, but the truth must be told. Facing starvation, the campers at Tum Tum make a decision that very few human beings have made. That decision turns Camp Tum Tum into... Cannibal Fat Camp!

## "Tales of Questionable Taste"
### John Bruni

For fans of the bizarre, the weird, the strange, StrangeHouse Books brings you a whirlwind of eighteen tales sure to amuse, confuse, horrify and leave you questioning your lack of taste. From the warped synapses of John Bruni come stories of the destruction of earth, via a humongous totally nude man in space, a portal to another dimension inside of an office worker's desk, a sordid love affair between two nefarious euthanasia enthusiasts, and many other yarns that span from psychological terror, to comedy, to downright disgusting!

**Now Available at StrangehouseBooks.com!**

# BEER RUN OF THE DEAD
## CHAPTER 3
### CHAOS IN CHRONOLOGICAL ORDER

Jefferson, the only black man in the room, stands amongst generals, congressman, and the President. He inserts a disc into a computer and a gigantic screen, which previously held a map of the world, now shows a video feed from somewhere just outside Earth's atmosphere.

"Gentlemen, as you know," Jefferson says, "we have a black-ops bio-weapons space lab deemed too dangerous to operate on Earth."

General Warren Peters speaks up, "The Pale Horse project?"

"Correct," Jefferson continues. "If just one of these viruses were to be released, gentlemen, we would be looking at millions, possibly billions of deaths. It would be Armageddon."

"Jefferson, get to the point," says the President.

Jefferson nods, clicks the video on. "Today, the Iranians made history by sending their first man to the moon... It was a total facade. They somehow gained the coordinates and successfully attacked the Pale Horse Space Station. This is the last recorded video from the weapons lab."

The video shows Earth below as it turns slowly on its axis. A rocket escapes the atmosphere. Then, from the nose of the rocket a capsule detaches and heads straight towards the camera's point of view.

The capsule then opens up and reveals a suicide bomber in a space suit. His chest is wrapped with dynamite, his helmet is covered with a turban, and he is carrying a megaphone in one hand and a detonator in the other.

As the suicide bomber hurtles towards the camera, we hear *ah la la la la la la la!*

There's a flash, then static.

"Jesus Christ, has the media gotten a hold of this yet?"

"Yes sir. We're stalling them now, telling them it was a collision of satellites. The explosion and fallout could be seen across the Midwest, and a chunk of the station struck a passenger jet before falling into a heavily populated area of St. Louis... Luckily, massive thunderstorms are clouding most of the visibility. A quarantine team has been mobilized but we believe it is too late. As of now we are successfully jamming broadcasts from Iran; they are already declaring victory."

There are wide-eyed stares across the conference table. People fidget in their clothes. Loosen their ties.

"How much time do we have?"

"About thirty minutes sir. We have to evacuate immediately to one of the underground bunkers. We are hoping that any residual viruses were burned up in the reentry through the atmosphere. But one in particular is troubling us."

General Peters says, "The Lazarus virus..."

Jefferson wipes sweat from his brow. "Yes sir, there has been no effective way found to stop the virus, besides complete nuclear incineration. Once it hits the air, it will begin to replicate out of control."

The conference room is as silent as a tomb for a

moment.

"Before we go," says the President, "Nuke the bastards. I want Iran so radioactive even cockroaches lose their goddamn teeth."

## II

Ol' Saint Louis. It's starting to rain. Somewhere a man-child Kip Evans sleeps a dreamless drug induced sleep. His mother and her new semen delivery system are dressed for a night on the town and they are driving, and doing some heavy petting.

Not far off two paramedics are pulling into a hospital. Headlights cut through the rain, lighting splotches of alabaster across cold brown stones, but their sirens are off. The man in the back, covered in a white sheet; he's dead. Multiple gunshot wounds in the chest. There's no rush.

They're pulling the corpse out on a gurney when an orderly in scrubs comes out to greet them. He's a big black guy. Russ. He's got a perfect mustache and sideburns. Big smile.

"Hey Russ. Busy night?"

"Damn right. That's the third one tonight. We got so many popsicles down there we're running out of room."

"Want us to give you a hand with that one?"

"Nah, I got it. He don't weigh shit."

And then the evening sky begins to light up. Russ and the paramedics stop, look up into the storm. Something bright barrels through the clouds, glowing red and ominous. There's this sound, like an oncoming train.

A moment later it streaks out into the open, some gigantic tumbling fireball. It strikes the city in the distance, and the night turns bright as day for just a split second. The three men shield their eyes.

"Fuckin' Al Queda!" Russ screams in soprano.

The paramedics turn to look at Russ but he's already running back into the hospital. They turn back to the city. A mushroom cloud looms up through coils of smoke and fire.

"Well it doesn't get much worse than that."

Then, as if on cue, a 747 spirals out of the clouds, a wing missing. It falls like an awkward boomerang, trailing smoke, crashes somewhere behind a line of trees, and explodes.

The paramedics look at each other.

"I fucking quit," says one.

Russ hauls ass through the hospital, he stops at a nurse's station.

One of them says, "Was that thunder?"

Gasping for air, Russ babbles, "Fucking...Bombed the city! Fucking Al Queda!...Bitches run! Run for your lives!"

The nurses look at each other, cock their eye brows, they turn to ask Russ a question and he's gone, sprinting to the elevators.

*Ding!* The elevator opens. An old man and woman are standing inside. Russ grabs them by their collars and throws them into the hallway. As the doors slide shut he yells at them, "Run! Save your old white asses!"

*Ding!* The doors open. Russ runs down a hallway, past a sign that reads Morgue with an arrow below it.

He bursts in, bellowing, "Doc! Yo, Doc where the fuck are you?"

Around him are almost a dozen bodies, covered in white sheets, some in body bags, lying on gurneys. Russ power walks through them, heading to an office in the back.

A hand grabs his shoulder from behind.

Russ screams in surprise, spins in a circle to see the Doc, a plump white man with poodle like white hair. The Doc is eating a sandwich, wearing headphones and a grimy smock.

"Jesus, Doc!"

"What did I tell you about smoking that grass," says the Doc through a mouth full of roast beef and rye. "Makes you paranoid."

"I ain't smoking no grass," Russ yells, "the city just

got bombed! Didn't you hear that shit?! We gotta get out of here!"

Doc taps his head phones. "What do you mean the city was bombed? You saw this?"

"Yeah it fucking came out the sky like a comet! Get your shit man, c'mon!"

"Well if it's a bad as you say let's check the TV then, shall we?"

"All you gotta do is look outside! I ain't making this shit up!"

Unperturbed, the Doc walks to a small TV in the corner, turns it on. Only static greets him. "That's strange."

Just as the words fall from Doc's mouth, several of the bodies begin to twitch as if some electrical current pumps through them. The Doc and Russ turn to the commotion, befuddled looks on their faces. Then all the bodies begin to twitch, more and more violently. They shake the tables they lie upon, filling the morgue with a cacophony of clanking and creaking.

A corpse beside them slowly sits up. Its white sheet slides down, revealing a "Y" autopsy cut in its chest. There's a blank look on its face, but then it snaps its head towards Doc and Russ; its mouth drops open, and an inhuman guttural scream comes out.

"Oh fuck this!" Russ squeals and runs from the room.

Corpses all across the room are sitting up, some falling from the tables, their guts plopping wet and sickly on the floor. Fingers press outward against body bags, thuds and bangs come from the wall units meant to hold dead cargo.

The Doc steps forward to the screaming dead man. "That's impossible," the Doc says poking the dead man in the chest. "You're dead."

The corpse grabs Doc's hand, pulls it up to its mouth and chomps the finger off in one swift bite.

"*Aaaargh!*" The Doc stumbles back, looking at his bloody stump, screaming. He turns and a woman, half her body charred from road rash, stands there. She grabs him by the neck and they topple over. Her thumbs, like icy cold daggers begin to sink into his neck.

Through his blurred vision, Doc sees the bare limbs of cadavers shuffling towards him. He struggles, but it's no use. The dead pile on top of him. Their fingers dig into him as if he were mere play-doh. He can feel wriggling, clenching fingers and hands *inside* him, pulling, tearing, *stretching* his skin and innards. Gurgling blood, he watches his own intestines as they are pulled up and out into hungry and eager mouths.

Teeth tear away his flesh, cold fingers pop out his eyes...*plop, plop*... and he screams. Screams 'till the very end.

## III

A news van pulls up at the edge of an inferno. It has destroyed a whole city block. Two major hotels have collapsed into burning rubble, and a good portion of the surrounding buildings are catching fire. A wall of smoke rolls down the street and people run from it as if it were Godzilla. The reporters don't know it, but they're looking at the wreckage of the remaining hull of the Pale Horse Space Station.

"Get the cameras rolling!" This is a reporter, blonde, big breasted, decisive and in control. She runs her fingers through her hair. This is it, the day her career takes a big giant step into news reporter stardom. Talk show appearances, a book even, she can feel it in her bones, this is it.

"Cameras are rolling! We're not getting a signal!"

"Why the fuck not?!"

"I don't know! How the fuck should I know! It's like were being jammed or something!"

"That doesn't make sense! Vince, make-up now! Get the cameras on me, we'll record and send as soon as we have signal!"

Behind them fire trucks are rolling in, sirens blaring.

"How does my hair look?"

Down the road, a hefty guy wearing a Cardinals t-shirt is ordering some biscuits and gravy from a drive through fast food chain that serves breakfast all day. A few moments ago something big lit up the sky, and was followed by a thunderous roar, and even the ground trembled a bit; but Cardinals Fan was not concerned, his only worry was his growling belly. "Yeah, I need two orders of biscuits and gravy, two hash browns, a cinnamon twist, and a large Diet Coke."

"Is Pepsi alright?" says a crackling voice.

"What? No, I won't drink that shit. Give me a Sprite, instead."

"Is Sierra Mist ok?"

"Are you serious? What is this shit?"

"So a Sierra Mist?"

"No I said are you serious-"

"Sierra Mist, gotcha. So we have two biscuits and gravy and-"

"I don't want a goddamn Sierra Mist! Hey listen jackass I want a-"

An ambulance out on the street distracts Cardinals Fan. It's weaving in and out of traffic then collides with a car at an intersection. Glass explodes, metal crumples, and the car spins and hits another. The ambulance rolls to a stop.

"Frikkin' shit!" The Cardinals fan exclaims.

"Sorry sir, we don't carry Mr. Pibb."

The back doors of the ambulance burst open. A paramedic tumbles out, a naked and bloody man straddling his back. The naked guy is taking bites out of the paramedic. People stop, get out of their vehicles to go help.

The ambulance driver steps out from the driver's side, stumbles in a daze, and then is struck by a small foreign car that comes up to the scene too fast. His body flies through the air doing cartwheels, hits a stop sign and spins around it. He splits open, his intestines spill out, wet and gleaming man-spaghetti.

Several men are trying to pull the naked guy off the other paramedic and the naked fucker is biting them, scratching them like an animal.

"What the fuck is going on?"

"Excuse me sir, did you see say foot long hot dog?"

## V

Rock and Steady are laying their best game on a drunk chick who's bent over some hand railing puking her guts out. A couple hundred yards in the distance is an amphitheater. A cover band is going into a Sammy Hagar song. The crowd begins to cheer.

"Hey, baby," Steady says with a slight slur, "soon as you're done with that, we got some beer to get that taste out your mouth for you."

She holds up a middle finger for them.

"Damn girl," says Rock, nudging Steady. "That's exactly what we were thinking. Think you can handle two studs at once?"

The drunk chick starts laughing even though she's still vomiting.

"Dude, she sounds like Chewbacca!"

A whining, droning sound comes from above, loud enough that it tops the music. Rock and Steady look up, see the 747 spinning out of control. They follow its descent, turning to watch it collide with the stage of the amphitheater. A massive fireball erupts. The amphitheater disappears in a flash, sending shrapnel through the crowd and a hot whoosh of air that's almost solid.

A spinning metal piece of something zips right between Rock and Steady. They turn back to the drunk chick and she's split in half. Somehow she's still puking.

Rock and Steady give each other a high five and then run like hell. They stop at a beer kiosk; around them people are fleeing and screaming, but they get right to stealing a keg.

"Go! Go! Go!"

Dan is stuck on 270. Traffic backed up all the way into God's bright, shiny rainbow asshole. It's starting to storm and it doesn't look like they're going anywhere fast. Just a minute ago something lit up the sky. Dan took it for lightning. His son, Charlie, sitting in a car seat in the back asks him what it was.

"Just lightning, kiddo."

"Dad, can I ride Uncle George's four wheeler?" Charlie says uncle like *untle*, says George like *dorge*. Cute kid.

"Well, we're gonna have to ask mom about that, buddy." Dan taps his fingers on the steering wheel impatiently, takes a sip of his coffee.

"Mom's a cunt!"

Dan spits his coffee out across the windshield, turns back to Charlie, "Who taught you that word!?"

"Uncle George said mom was a cunt!" Charlie giggles.

"Charlie don't ever, ever say that word do you hear-"

Dan stops in mid sentence. Beside the road, several deer erupt from the tree line. Then a dog, then a cat, a rabbit and some squirrels.

"Ooooh look deers, dad! Deers!"

What follows doesn't make sense. Dan rubs his eyes.

*Are those bloody naked people? What in God's name...*

It's evident those people are chasing the animals, but as soon as they come out of the woods, the nude, grizzly figures stop together, almost like birds in a flock. They change their direction and make way straight for the traffic jam.

Dan finds himself rolling up the windows, locking the doors.

"Dad that man has no pants. I can see his weenie!" Charlie giggles.

"Charlie don't look at them!"

"Dad, booooobies!"

Dan looks around, the traffic is so bad he can't pull up, can't go backwards, its bumper to bumper gridlock. There are at least a dozen freaks coming up on the shoulder, some of them completely nude, some of them in hospital gowns. Dan blinks. Some of them have big "Y" cuts covered in stitches in their chests. They all have one thing in common though, bloody mouths, blood drenched hands.

*Is this some kind of joke?*

When a pale, blue veined woman, nude as the day she was born, with dead sunken eyes and tube sock tits (*Medusa Boobs, Dan thinks*), runs straight to Dan's driver's side window and smacks her bloody greasy face off it, he decides this is not a joke. Not a joke at all.

"Charlie, hold on!"

Dan throws the car into drive, punches the gas and rams the car ahead of him. It budges just enough that he can pull off onto the shoulder into the grass. The air fills with the sounds of much honking, like warning cries of some massive metal herd of steel and fiberglass beasts. Suddenly, there seems to be dozens of figures, crawling over cars, slamming into them, beating at the windows, and even in the car he can hear them, some strange chorus of ghoulish moans and wails.

The Medusa Boob lady tries to punch his window as Dan guns it. Behind him, Charlie is squealing. Dan can't tell if its terror or excitement, all Dan knows is that he suddenly, painfully wants to be far, far away from whatever the hell is happening.

And he's doing forty, then fifty in the grass beside the highway. He looks back in the rearview mirror, sees cars following his lead, sees Charlie with both hands thrown in the air as if he's on a roller coaster. What Dan doesn't see is the truck pull off the road in front of him.

Dan hits the side of that truck at over sixty miles an hour. His windshield shatters and comes out in one big piece and lands in the bed of the truck. The back of his car lifts from the ground from the sudden, violent halt.

The airbag hits Dan in the face as if you could put Mike Tyson into a balloon. Then Dan hears this sound;

*Weeeeeeeeeeeee!*

And it's Charlie. It's his son, catapulted from his car seat, flying through where the windshield should've been. Charlie flies, hands forward, a miniature superman, hits the cab of the truck with a thump and cart wheels into the air. All this, in a second or less.

*"Charlieeeeee!"*

And Charlie lands in someone's arms. Some miracle man, some angel sent from god to catch his son... and Dan realizes with a sinking horror so deep you couldn't fill it up with ten Titanics, that it isn't an angel at all. It's one of the freaks from the woods.

And Dan roars, because there's his son, being ripped to pieces in front of him. Ripped to pieces like how dogs fight over a piece of steak, or how kids fight over a doll.

## VII

Weezy didn't take no shit. That was for damn sure. And the punk ass bitch he just popped in the heart knew that now too. Knew it from hell. Punk-ass, yellow motherfucker had his chance. Punk Ass had enough blow he could have been somebody. Nope, Punk Ass snorted and smoked all that shit up. All he had to do was move some weight. Now that's all he was. Just some weight.

Weezy came and settled that score.

Weezy is about to scoot out of Punk Ass's apartment, he gets to the door and hears Punk Ass moan. Punk Ass twitches on the floor.

*Ah fuck,* Weezy thinks, *gonna have ta stomp this motherfucker's brains in.*

Weezy turns back, and there's Punk Ass sitting up. Punk Ass is looking him right in the eye. Punk Ass should know better.

Weezy raises his pistol, shoots Punk Ass in the chest. Punk Ass, he takes the bullet, his body turns with the force of it, but he don't stop looking at Weezy. He doesn't stop trying to get up.

*Motherfucker must be high as shit.*

Weezy don't have time for this. Weezy unloads the clip into Punk Ass's chest. The gunshot is so loud in the apartment, Weezy is sure he's got permanent hearing loss. And here's Punk Ass getting up on his feet.

Weezy knows a high ass motherfucker can take some punishment, but this is some bullshit. Weezy also knows he's done spent too much time here as it is, fired too many shots. But he's gotta take this motherfucker down for sure. Dead men don't name drop, but a half dead punk-ass will.

And look at this, Punk Ass wants to fight. He's stumbling right for Weezy.

"Oh you wanna fight bitch?"

And Punk Ass takes a punch in the mouth, his teeth cut deep into Weezy's knuckles…

## VIII

The streets are alive with the dead and the living. The city's on fire, the dead on patrol.

A man in a red jacket yells *Go Cards* and bunts a bloody freak in the face with a baseball bat. Then a man kicks him in the balls from behind and yells *Go Cubs,* then steals his wallet and shoes and runs cackling into the shadows.

Two cops are on a sidewalk, wrestling with a perp. People are running to and fro around them in the rain. A young guy runs up, sees the cops trying to cuff the perp' on the ground. His head twists around looking, and then, the young guy jumps in the cop car and takes off.

"Sonuvabitch!" one of the cops yells. He pulls his pistol and starts firing. 9mm rounds streak through the crowd and people drop shrieking, a lucky shot zips through the driver's side window and into the cheek of the car-jacker. Blood and teeth and part of his nose spray across the windshield of the cruiser and his body jerks the wheel violently, right into a crowd of Asian kids. Their bodies fly, skid across the asphalt, crumple underneath the car.

A woman is standing on a balcony looking down. Back in the room, a group of deranged cannibals are slowly but surely caving her hotel room door in. One of them is her husband. He'd gone into the hallway to check out a commotion only to find an elderly woman eating the throat out of a bellhop. Her husband, being the Samaritan he was, tried to pull the old woman off the poor bastard who was clutching his neck, convulsing on the floor. As she watched on in frozen terror from her doorway, watched her husband grapple with the crazy lady, the bellhop bled out, shit his pants and laid still.

"Susan," her husband yelled. "Call security!"

She couldn't move. She had never seen so much blood. Never saw anyone die. Never saw anyone *murdered.*

"Susan now!"

By the time she had stumbled back in the room on shaky legs, and found the phone, and found the line to be busy, the bellhop had returned to life, un-life, and was helping the old crazy lady eat chunks of her husband.

Susan had stepped back in the doorway; saw her husband screaming, half his face torn off. He was viciously beating the old lady in the face, and trying to kick the bellhop off of him at the same time.

Somehow through the fight he managed to yell, "Susan, get back! Lock the fucking door!"

She cried, she wailed but she did as she was told. And now she's standing on the balcony, looking four stories down, wondering which was worse; to be eaten alive or to jump to your death?

She steps onto the ledge, behind her the door shatters. Wind pulls at her auburn hair, smoke and ash flutter through the night around her. She hears footsteps, and she closes her eyes. Susan leaps, and screams all the way down, her dress fluttering up above her head.

Below a crack-head is running for dear life with a box of pizza, a pineapple and Canadian bacon pizza. Susan lands, her ass enveloping his face, and pile drives the crack head's melon with such force into the sidewalk that his head explodes.

Susan's ass and legs are sore, but somehow she's alive. She gets up, pulls a slice of pizza from between her legs and joins the flow of fleeing people.

A National Guard unit has set up a road block. They fire willy-nilly into a horde of people that just won't die.

"Aim for the head, goddammit!"

A soldier unclips a grenade from his vest, pulls the pin and lobs it into the crowd. It bounces off the skull of a freak with a dull *thunk*. The grenade rolls off somewhere underneath a car and explodes. The roar is deafening, the car lifts into the air and lands on its side, smashing freaks beneath its weight. Bodies drop in the flash, some caught by the force so hard they become only wet splats on the walls of surrounding buildings. But the horde does not stop, they run forward, undeterred by bullets or bombs or pain.

A stripper named Candy is snorting coke off the back of a toilet seat. It's been a long day. Her legs and knees are sore and some perv' had squeezed her titty so hard it had a knot in it. She still has four hours left on her shift, so she figures a big rail of blow will set things straight and give her the strength to carry on.

The cocaine, some good shit hardly stepped on or cut, enters her nose, hits her mucus membrane and she shudders in a sudden euphoria. And then, she can't breathe, she clutches her heart and sinks to the floor. Through the pain and panic, she knows she just went too far. She's overdosed right on the locker room floor.

Several minutes later another stripper, Danny, walks in. She finds Candy standing in the corner, her shoulders slumped. "Candy baby," says Danny, "what's wrong?"

Candy turns her head. Danny sees blood dribbling down from her nose, across her lips and chin. Candy moans, her lips pull back in a snarl.

"Damn, girl," Danny says, "you're all fucked up!"

Candy stumbles forward, her hands straight ahead. She grabs one of Danny's tits.

"Bitch," Danny laughs, "you're such a fucking freak!"

Then Candy bites Danny's nipple off, and Danny isn't laughing anymore.

Made in the USA
Middletown, DE
20 July 2015